BRIE'S SUBMISSION

Love Me

Red Phoenix

Dedication

More love to MrRed!
My lover, my mate, and my Sir.

A huge thank-you to my peeps who've continue to
believe in Brie and help me to spread her message of self-
discovery – Brandi (my awesome cover designer) and
Becki & Marilyn (my tireless proofers)

And nothing but gratitude for all my incredible fans!

SIGN UP FOR MY NEWSLETTER HERE FOR THE LATEST RED PHOENIX UPDATES

FOLLOW ME ON INSTAGRAM
INSTAGRAM.COM/REDPHOENIXAUTHOR

SALES, GIVEAWAYS, NEW RELEASES, PREORDER LINKS, AND MORE! SIGN UP HERE
REDPHOENIXAUTHOR.COM/NEWSLETTER-SIGNUP

CONTENTS

A Little Girl Time

B rie looked over at Mary, formerly known as Blonde Nemesis, while she sipped on her gin martini. She'd taken the girls to a local joint with cheap drinks and a casual atmosphere for their feminine 'debriefing' after the second auction. The bartender was a friend of Brie's, so he made their drinks strong in appreciation of her patronage. It wasn't a sexy hangout spot by any means, but they could chat in their long coats—which covered their school uniforms—and no one would question it or bother them.

Tonight was all about sharing the little details only girls share with each other. However, Brie had invited Mary, and that choice seemed to be stifling the conversation. She decided a few personal (but not too deep) questions might help the girl to open up. "So Mary, I heard that you work in a pharmacy. What made you decide on that career choice?"

It was such a basic question, but it got a bizarre response. Mary turned beet red and twitched in her seat. Then she grabbed her rum and Coke and downed half of it. "It's stupid. I don't want to talk about it."

Lea crinkled her brow in disgust. "Seriously, you won't even talk about that? You suck."

Mary remarked snidely, "I suck better than you, Gagalicious."

Brie slammed her fist on the bar counter. "That's enough, Mary. I brought you along because I wanted to get to know you and have a few laughs. But if you plan on being a bitch the whole night, then leave. Lea and I don't need that shit."

Mary put her hands in the air in a mocking sign of surrender. "Whoa, don't get your panties in a wad there, Brie."

Lea held up her glass threateningly. "You'd better leave now if you don't want this drink in your face."

Mary gathered her purse and stood up, but then she settled back in her chair. She quickly finished off her drink and asked the bartender for another one. "Oh, and get these girls whatever they want…and double it." She added with a smirk, "Apparently, they need to be drunk to stand me."

"Are you going to behave?" Brie asked.

"Yes, Miss Bennett."

Brie relaxed a little and gave Lea a nudge with her shoulder. "You can put your drink down, Lea." Then she addressed Mary. "So why did you choose to be a pharmacist?"

"If you must know, I became a pharmacist because of the movie *It's a Wonderful Life*."

Lea lifted her glass up again and growled, "What? Do you have to make a joke about everything? Brie just asked you a serious question."

Mary snapped, "I *am* being serious, damn it. And if you give me a hard time I'm going to punch one of your fake boobs!"

Brie quickly scootched her stool in between the two of them. "Okay, so how did an old Christmas movie make you want to become a pharmacist?"

Mary huffed irritably before answering. "You know the scene where the pharmacist accidentally gives the wrong medication that could have killed the child? Well, when I saw that growing up, I knew that's what I wanted to be because I would *never* make that mistake. In my mind, a dedicated pharmacist is an unsung hero."

"I definitely never thought of it that way before," Lea commented, sipping her drink instead of splashing it over Mary.

"But aren't you too young to be a pharmacist?" Brie asked, knowing it took years of extra schooling.

"I graduated early." She shrugged indifferently. "It's not a big deal if you're smart and motivated."

Brie looked at her rival with more respect. "Who would guess an old black and white movie could inspire someone's life?" She stared directly into Mary's eyes, wanting her to know she was being sincere when she added, "I don't think you should be embarrassed about your reasons for wanting to be a pharmacist. It shows an intriguing side to your character." Brie clinked her glass against Mary's and took a sip.

Lea leaned in, instantly changing the subject. "So, what do you guys think of Marquis Gray?"

"It's easy to see what *you* think," Mary said, rolling

her eyes. "Don't think we aren't aware of all those lusty stares you give the man."

"Am I that obvious?" Lea asked in concern.

Brie nodded. "The only reason I consented to a flogging was the way you looked at him after he 'punished' you."

Lea blushed a nice shade of pink, all the way down to her overabundant cleavage. "Oh, but he does know how to whip a girl. I'm grateful for any session I get with Marquis."

Brie shuddered pleasantly, remembering her own experience. "He *is* quite talented with the flogger." Then she frowned and added, "Although…his dark eyes scare me. It's as if they see straight into my soul and discover things even *I* don't know about myself. It's freaky."

Mary grumbled, "I don't know what is wrong with that man. He hasn't shown any interest in teaching me, and I'm obviously the one who wants what he has to offer."

Brie was afraid to share her thoughts, knowing how sensitive Mary was about her past. She was certain Marquis Gray didn't want to train Mary until she had worked through the unresolved issues stemming from her violent childhood.

Lea jumped back in and asked, "What about Ms. Clark?"

"She's a bitch," Brie answered.

"Hear, hear!" Mary lifted her glass.

Lea looked uncomfortable and took a quick sip of her drink.

Brie's eyes widened. "No *way*!"

"No way, what?" Mary snorted.

Brie shook her head in disbelief when she asked, "Lea, you don't have a crush on Ms. Clark, do you?"

Lea grinned and shrugged. "What if I do? Ms. Clark is hot! I mean, you saw her blonde pussy up close, Brie. Isn't that the prettiest thing you've ever seen? I was so jealous when Sir asked you to join her on stage."

"Are you kidding me, Lea? Eating her was one of the hardest things I've ever done." When Brie saw her friend's hurt expression, she quickly added, "But she does have a damn cute pussy."

"If you're talking hot then you must be talking about Sir," Mary purred. "That man… Finest cock I have *ever* had."

Brie felt her jealousy rise up like bile. She was about to rain down her feminine fury on Blondie when Lea spoke up. "You may have had Sir's cock, but it's easy to see Brie has his heart."

Mary sputtered, "You're wrong. Sure…he may have had a thing for her…but it's over and done. Heck, he barely looks at her now."

Good, Brie thought. At least Mary was clueless about their true feelings. Maybe the trainers were equally oblivious. *Well, all of them except Marquis Gray.*

Desperate to change the subject, Brie mentioned Master Coen. "Have you ever seen so many muscles before?"

Mary took the bait and commented, "Shit, he looks like Mr. Universe. I just wanted to lick all those muscles when I was on top of him."

"You know, I don't think he is all that sexy," Brie

told her. "Sure, I like muscles, but not *muscles*. It's too much."

"Are you nuts?" Lea asked, her jaw hanging open. "Of all three men, he is the best looking. Whenever he takes his shirt off, I almost come." She wiggled in her seat playfully. "Seriously, every time."

"To each their own, I guess," Brie answered, smiling into her glass as she took a sip. She wasn't sure how either girl could think anyone held a candle to Sir.

Lea seemed to know it was pointless to argue about Sir with Brie, so she asked, "What do you think this week's classes are going to be about?"

"You got me," Brie replied. She looked at Mary, who didn't say a word. The girl downed her drink and signaled the bartender for a new one. Both Brie and Lea could tell she was keeping a secret, and bugged her relentlessly until she spilled what she knew.

"You two are irritating like little Chihuahuas—yip, yip, yip. Fine. Enough already, I'll tell you. I overheard Ms. Clark talking to Marquis Gray. I think we're going to have a week of bondage."

Brie's heart did a flip. *A whole week of bondage?* It was a dream come true! Up to this point, she had only experienced light bondage, but the thought of diving deeper made her loins wet. "Are you sure?" she asked, not wanting to be disappointed.

"Clark was speaking about bondage to him after class on Thursday. She said something about not pushing one of us too far. Marquis Gray seemed to disagree. Something tells me one of us is going to have *quite* a week ahead…and I'm hoping it is me." Mary signaled again to the bartender, looking impatient. "You guys need another?"

They both declined, but Lea remarked, "I think you could drink both of us under the table."

"No doubt. You two are pussies." Mary gave the bartender a flirtatious wink when she finally got his attention, and Brie couldn't help noticing John's lustful stare.

"This one's on the house," he announced when he handed Mary her new drink.

"Thanks, Hotcheeks," Mary purred.

John grinned as he walked to the other side of the counter to take care of a regular. Although Brie had often flirted with John and considered him *her* bartender, it appeared he preferred blondes. *Figures…*

Lea watched the exchange and then looked at Brie knowingly. She leaned over and asked, "Wanna know what I heard?"

"What?"

She said in a solemn voice, "Continually blowing out the candle your Dom lights during wax play can have negative results."

Brie cracked a grin. Lea was always good for a joke. "Oh, yeah? Well, I heard that when your Dom drops his whip it's unwise to sing, 'Missed me, missed me, now you gotta kiss me.'"

Lea broke out in genuine laughter and Brie joined in, reveling in their easy friendship. When they'd quieted down, both looked over at Mary, waiting for her to add to the jovial moment. Mary shifted in her seat, looking upwards as she tried to pull something out of her head.

"Okay, okay, I've got one. I heard that adding Sir or Mistress to 'Are you fucking kidding me?' may be interpreted as a death wish."

"Nice," Lea complimented. "Oh, that's a definite keeper."

When it was time to leave, Brie invited both girls to her place to film their thoughts about that past week for her documentary.

"Are you insane?" Mary bristled. "There is no way I would let you record me. Go to hell." Her response didn't necessarily surprise Brie—that girl was all kinds of closed doors.

"Suit yourself, Mary," Lea answered gleefully. "I can't wait to find out all the juicy details of Brie's time with Doctor Harris."

"Oooh, and I can't wait to find out what having a Domme is like." Brie turned to Lea and asked, "What *was* she like, anyway?"

"I'm not saying a word until we get to your place." Lea grinned at Mary impishly. "Ta-ta, Mary. You don't know what you're missing."

The two headed to her apartment, leaving Mary behind. On the drive there, Brie reflected that Blondie still had a long way to go before she would truly be one of the team, but tonight had been a decent start. Mary's line of, "Are you fucking kidding me, Sir?" would play in Brie's mind from now on whenever she wanted to say no to her Doms.

Even better was Mary's revelation that this week they would be focusing on bondage lessons. Brie quivered in excitement at the delightful opportunities waiting ahead.

The Call of the Rope

As Brie walked towards the Training Center on Monday, she shook her head. Blue Eyes—her pet name for Todd Wallace—was there at the front door again. He'd been there every day, waiting for her and, just like the times before, he pushed open the door and let her pass with a simple, "Good evening, Miss Bennett."

She nodded and tried to walk past him, but a crowd of students rushed through the door, propelling her against his chest. She noticed Todd had a manly smell—one that inspired a feeling of intense sexuality. It made her heart flutter. She mumbled a quick apology without looking at him, then headed towards the elevator as quickly as her six-inch heels would allow.

Once the elevator doors had closed, Brie took a couple of deep breaths to calm her rapidly beating heart. No way was she going to let that boy complicate her life. She had plenty of experienced Doms to tease and please her. A lowly business student didn't stand a chance against them.

By the time the elevator doors opened, she had regained her composure. *Now for the real fun!* she thought as she walked into Mr. Gallant's classroom. She waved at both Lea and Mary as she sat down. It felt a little strange to see Mary's lips curve upwards in an attempt at a smile. It wasn't natural; even Mary seemed to think so, and her 'smile' quickly disappeared.

Mr. Gallant cleared his throat and started class before the bell, as per the norm. "I was pleased to see your ratings from this last auction. It's an improvement over last week, and highlights your continued progress. Well done, ladies."

Mr. Gallant handed Brie her evaluation first. "Another seven. A nice, solid performance, Miss Bennett." She took the packet but waited to look through it, wanting to hear the other girls' scores.

"Miss Wilson, Sir Edwards gave you a six. A marked improvement over last week." He handed out the last one to Lea. "Ms. Taylor, you also received a six from your Domme, Mistress White. Please look over their ratings and learn from them."

Brie looked through the pages. 'Beautifully unwilling, but unfailingly obedient. Focused on pleasing her Master.' 'Deep-throat skills above expected.' 'Found her to be a fascinating individual able to hold an intelligent conversation, as well as my cock in her mouth—lovely.' Brie searched through it again to find her weaknesses, but only found, 'Throat was irritated, should rest for a couple of days.'

She was curious as to why she had only received a seven if he'd had no complaints. Her question was soon answered when an assistant walked into the room and handed Mr. Gallant an apple.

Her teacher looked at it curiously, and then walked over to her desk and gave it to Brie. "Apparently, Master Harris wanted you to have this."

She took the red apple tied with a black bow, noting it had a small card bearing her name attached. She opened the envelope and read the contents.

Miss Bennett, enjoy the apple. It is my little reminder for you NOT to irritate your throat for another twenty-four hours. Doctor's orders. I personally would have rated you higher, but it is frowned upon at the Center. (We wouldn't want new subs to get big heads.)

Brie blushed and slipped the card into her coat pocket.

"What did he say?" Mr. Gallant asked.

"He wants me not to deep-throat today because of my irritated throat."

Mr. Gallant frowned slightly. "Odd… Miss Bennett, do you feel a deeper connection was made between you two?"

Lea gasped softly. Brie looked over in her direction, suddenly aware of her friend's feelings towards the good doctor. Lea hadn't mentioned anything, but it was easy to read on her face now.

Brie answered Mr. Gallant truthfully. "No, I'm not into doctors and he knows that." She could see Lea visibly relax. How adorable that her friend had a crush on Master Harris. She could see the two making a good pair because of their shared sense of humor and similar tastes in kink.

"I will begin the class, then. I want to start by asking the same question I did last week. Do you think there is such a thing as the 'perfect sub'?"

Lea raised her hand and was quickly called on. "Yes, I believe if I work really hard I can become the perfect sub."

Mr. Gallant turned to Brie. "Do you agree, Miss Bennett?"

Her heart said yes, but she knew better based on the tone of his voice. "No."

He raised an eyebrow. "And why not?"

Crap! So much for faking it. She stalled for time as she scrambled to produce an intelligent answer. "I believe you can work hard to improve your skills. If you do that, you will succeed in being proficient..." She glanced at Mr. Gallant. His eyebrow was still raised, as if he knew she was bullshitting. "However, being the perfect sub..." She had to dig deep, but then it came to her. "No, there is no such thing."

"Why not?"

"Each person is different. Our strengths and weaknesses can't fit everyone." She tilted her head slightly as she spoke, "I am not sure if you would agree, Mr. Gallant, but I think it is possible to be the perfect sub for one person... Maybe even more than one person. However, it's impossible to be everything to everyone and still be true to yourself."

He nodded and turned to Mary. "What are your

thoughts, Miss Wilson?"

Mary answered immediately. "She pretty much stole what I was going to say."

Yeah, right!

"Aren't you striving to become the perfect sub, Miss Wilson?"

She stammered, "Well, I can't be, so why bother?"

"So, you are *not* attempting to become the perfect sub?"

"No, wait—I want to be the perfect sub!" she blurted.

"Which is it, Miss Wilson?"

Brie liked how Mr. Gallant wouldn't let his students off with half-assed answers.

"I want to be better than any other sub here," she answered defiantly.

"Will that make you the perfect sub?"

She looked down at her lap. "No, I guess it won't. But at least I will be better than everyone else."

Mr. Gallant's next comment seemed offhand, but was scorching. "I wonder if an arrogant sub truly understands the lifestyle." He didn't wait for an answer from her and dove right into his topic. "This week we are exploring bondage."

Brie silently cheered.

He walked to the front of the class and pulled down a white screen. "There are many different bondage materials that can be used. I will be teaching you about the most common, as well as those that are unsafe and should be avoided."

Brie got out her paper and pencil, eager to discover

all she could about her favorite subject.

Mr. Gallant turned on the projector and pointed to the first object. "Handcuffs seem to be one of the first items the uninformed envision when they think of bondage. These restraint devices are limiting and can cause abrasions if the submissive struggles. However, they do have a pleasant visual and psychological effect, so if they are going to be used I recommend purchasing a professional set with a lock that prevents them from tightening further."

Brie did not consider the feel of metal cuffs to be a turn-on and wrote beside her notes, *Not for me.*

"They should never be used for suspension," he added.

Lea raised her hand and waited for Mr. Gallant to call on her. "What is suspension?"

He smiled. "Good question, Ms. Taylor. It is the act of binding a submissive so that no part of her body touches the floor."

Brie trembled inside. *What would that feel like?*

Mr. Gallant continued, "Leather laces are best used for decorative binding, as they are often thin and can cut into the skin. Leather also shrinks when wet."

Rytsar had used leather on Brie during her fantasy, but he had untied her at different points when he'd known she would struggle. His experience had made it a safer option. Next to leather she wrote, *Only with experienced Doms.*

"I would highly discourage the use of pantyhose and plastic clothesline rope. You want to use items that will not cut into the skin or be difficult to remove afterwards." Next to those, she wrote, *Nope, nope, nope!*

"Nylon rope is a good choice because of its smooth texture and availability, but mountain climbing web is also an excellent choice and provides the Dom with a variety of colors to choose from."

When he clicked to the next picture, Brie was surprised to see something that looked like duct tape. "One extremely easy material to use is bondage tape. It does not stick to the skin and comes in many colors as well. The number of wraps determines the strength of the bonds. It can be reused but must be cleaned after each use."

Brie struggled not to smile as she wrote down, *Oh, please, yes!*

"A common and suitable restraint is the leather cuff, which can be attached to chains, special tables, chairs or spreader bars. It allows for total creativity for the Dom without worries about safety."

Brie hesitantly raised her hand. Mr. Gallant called on her. "Yes, Miss Bennett?"

"What's a spreader bar?"

He smiled slightly when he answered. "A spreader bar is a useful piece of equipment that spreads the sub's appendages apart for total restraint."

Brie nodded and wrote next to cuffs and spreaders, *Could be fun.*

"The last I will talk about today is jute. It is a natural fiber that is often used in the Japanese art of Kinbaku." The picture on the screen showed a naked woman hanging in the air, suspended by rope tied in intricate knots. "It is a type of bondage where the rope and the sub become a piece of art, literally beautiful bondage. It takes both skill and time for a Dom to become a baku-shi, or rope master."

Brie remembered Mary talking about the weird way Tono had tied her up, and she suddenly wondered if he was a bakushi artist. Oh, if he was, Brie desperately wanted to experience his expertise! Next to jute, she wrote, *Hoping and dreaming.*

"Bondage speaks to the trust a submissive puts in her Dom and is an exquisite representation of that release of power in visual form. A Dom is aroused by the knowledge that his sub cannot physically prevent his desires from playing out…which is a heady feeling indeed," Mr. Gallant added with a glint in his eye. "However, the true allure behind bondage is the freedom the submissive has to embrace her forbidden desires under the guise of helplessness."

His words resonated in Brie's heart. *Yes!* She wanted to be tied down so she could freely enjoy those things she hadn't dared to surrender to before. Butterflies played in her stomach when Mr. Gallant dismissed the class and told them to proceed to the practicums.

During her practicum, Brie was asked to join Master Coen on the stage. She had never had a scene with the muscular trainer before and was nervous, since she knew he did not want her in the program.

A large desk had been placed on the stage, similar in style to a teacher's desk. Master Coen took off his shirt, exposing his ripped muscles and tanned chest. Brie instantly thought of Lea and wondered if she was close to coming. It was difficult not to laugh, but she managed to keep a straight face as she stared at the floor.

"Take off your thong and lay your stomach against the desk. I am going to show you the pleasure of a good spanking, Miss Bennett."

Brie couldn't help noticing his bulging arm muscles, and swallowed anxiously as she removed her panties.

"You have been a troubled student and must be properly punished." His tone was teasing, which eased her nerves somewhat.

Brie lay on the desk with her cheek pressed against the cool wood. She felt Master Coen lift her microskirt, exposing her naked ass. He rubbed it gently without saying a word. Then he walked around to the front of the desk and opened a drawer. He pulled out a metal two-foot pole about an inch in diameter with cuffs attached to either end. He laid it down in front of her. Next, he pulled out a roll of black tape and put it beside the bar. Master Coen walked back behind her again and quietly commanded, "Spread your legs apart."

Brie had not suspected she would be made to wear a spreader bar so soon. Her breathing increased as she did his bidding. He took the bar from the desk and fastened one leather cuff to her ankle. She was surprised and relieved to feel the cuff was lined with fur. He adjusted it to fit snugly. He moved her other foot to the desired distance and attached the second cuff. Brie could imagine how sexy she must look with six-inch heels, a naked ass, and a spreader bar between her ankles. She wiggled her butt, just for fun.

But her stomach did a flip when he stood up. She was suddenly aware how powerless she felt now that she could no longer close her legs. What had seemed sexy in her head was proving to be challenging in real life.

He ran his hands over her round ass cheeks again, murmuring, "Wayward students must take their punishments with grace. Do you understand, Miss Bennett?"

"Yes, Master Coen," Brie answered, her limbs trembling slightly.

"Put your hands behind your back."

She crossed her wrists behind the middle of her back. She felt completely immobilized when he bound them together with the bondage tape.

"Would you prefer to be gagged?"

"No, Master Coen."

"Excellent. I do enjoy the verbal sounds that go along with a proper spanking." Brie felt weak all over. "As this is your first time, I will acclimate your body and mind to the stimulation. You are allowed to cry if you must, but not beg. Until the spanking is over, the only word you may speak is the safe word. Nod your head if you understand."

Brie's cheek stuck to the desk when she attempted to nod. She tensed when she felt his hand on her buttocks again. "You've been quite the challenge, Miss Bennett," he growled, his voice laced with lust. Instead of hurting her, his hand caressed the swell of her ass and her inner thighs. It felt nice and soon she found herself warming up to his caresses.

"Such a spankable ass," he stated. "I must heed its call."

Her whole body stiffened, but the smack he gave her was light and pleasing. She relaxed slightly and concentrated on the sensations he was creating. Master Coen continued to lightly slap her on the ass; first one side then the other, lower then higher until every square inch of her shapely butt had been spanked. Without warning, he landed a harder blow. The sound of it echoed through the auditorium, followed by her surprised cry.

He caressed the burning area. "Accept your punishment." The caressing continued until he slapped her other ass cheek with the same force. She cried out, but his soothing touch immediately followed and eased the burn.

"Color?"

"Green, Master Coen."

"Good. Now I am going to spank you hard four times. Count them in your head."

His large hand landed on her ass, taking her breath away. It was immediately followed by a similar smack on her other ass cheek, and then another higher up, and the last at the same level on the original cheek. It burned, but the sting did not last long because of his gentle caresses.

"Your ass is starting to look properly pink, Miss Bennett." His fingers glided down the valley of her buttocks to her aching pussy. He played with her outer lips and teased her moist entrance with his fingers. Brie moaned softly and wiggled against his hand, surprised by how turned on she'd become by his corporal punishment. He continued to tease her, alternating between spanking and caressing her bottom—creating anticipation and longing.

"You have proved a repentant student. A set of ten, and then I will take you," he announced. "Are you ready?"

Brie tensed but nodded obediently. His hand danced over the curve of her ass, tickling her just before it spanked her warm skin. She grunted this time, wondering if she could handle all ten. The next smack landed with equal vigor and a gasp escaped her lips. By the eighth one, tears were running down her cheeks unchecked. The last was the hardest and loudest of them all, but it sent a pleasurable shockwave through her groin.

He stroked her fiery skin, murmuring quietly, "Nicely done, Miss Bennett. Nicely done."

Master Coen gently lifted her by the waist and she put her knees on the desk. He helped Brie to tuck her legs underneath herself. She felt deliciously helpless with her red little ass in the air, her legs bound by the spreader bar and her wrists tied behind her. She heard him unzip his pants and looked back. Master Coen had a large, veiny cock, just like the rest of his body. He placed his hands on her warm buttocks and eased himself inside her. His throbbing shaft filled her to capacity.

The heat from her wet pussy caused him to groan. "You seem to have enjoyed our little spanking session." He caressed and squeezed her still burning ass as he thrust his sizeable manhood inside her. "Nothing like fucking a beautiful girl with freshly spanked tush."

She closed her eyes and ignored the ache of the bindings as her trainer took her hard. Her restricted movement made her his play toy, and for some reason that excited her. She started moaning as the sexual pressure built to an unbearable peak. His cock was rubbing her in just the right place, but she was afraid to orgasm without permission.

Brie panted, "May I come, Master Coen?"

"Do you feel a troublemaker deserves to orgasm?" he growled lustfully.

"If…it…pleases you," she gasped out.

In answer, he grabbed her thighs and rammed deep into her hungry depths. "Because you took your punishment well, Miss Bennett, you may."

She cried out in pleasure and delicious release as her pussy clamped down on his cock. Her bindings and stinging ass were forgotten as she climaxed hard and long. His orgasm soon followed, creaming her with his essence. He pulled away slowly, then carefully undid the cuffs on each ankle and unwound the tape binding her wrists. She felt stiff all over as he helped her off the desk and turned her to face the panel.

"How would you rate the scene, Miss Bennett?" Sir asked. His eyes glimmered with excitement, which in turn thrilled Brie.

"I would give it an eight, Sir."

"Does that surprise you?" Marquis Gray asked.

"I suppose it shouldn't have, Marquis Gray, given the scene you and I shared with the flogger. But yes, I am surprised there is something sensual about the combination of being caressed and spanked."

Ms. Clark followed up with her own question. "What is your opinion of the spreader bar?"

"It's a scary piece of equipment because it makes me feel so helpless," Brie answered. She glanced at Master Coen and then remarked with a shy grin, "I guess that's also part of its charm."

Her female trainer actually *smiled* at her. "You handled the scene well. Of course, Master Coen did take it easy on you. Still, it was pleasant to watch."

"Thank you, Ms. Clark," Brie answered, trying to hide her surprise. It was a pleasant shock not to be on the woman's bad side, for once.

At the end of the night, Sir explained that the week ahead would not only include a variety of bondage scenarios, but that each girl was going to be stretched and challenged in areas previously uncharted. He looked directly at Brie, adding, "We expect you to use your safe word when the need arises this week, for we will be focusing on finding the edge of your limits, here in the safety of the Center."

Brie returned Sir's unwavering gaze, trying to appear far braver than she felt.

Fire and Ice

Brie was nervous the next day when she pulled up to the school. Sir had pretty much warned her that she was going to be using her safe word, which meant something difficult would be ahead. The only thing that made it bearable was knowing that the trainers wanted to help her to grow fully as a submissive, and would not allow anything harmful to happen.

She actually smiled when she saw Blue Eyes at the door. She was growing accustomed to their daily interactions, grateful that they only required a nod of her head. He swung the door open and let her pass. "You're looking especially fine tonight."

She blanched a little. That was not his normal greeting. She pulled the belt tighter around her coat and continued on as if she hadn't heard him. *Why did he have to ruin it by saying something new?* Brie snuck a glance back, wondering what he was up to, but all his attention was focused on a group of chatty girls who were walking through the door.

Brie shook it off and hurried to class.

Mr. Gallant gave the girls time to write another fantasy in their journals. She opened the luxurious book with glee. The words she wrote on the gold-lined pages now had a chance of becoming reality. She shivered in excitement as she penned another favorite fantasy:

I was taken from my parents at the age of twelve to live in the temple. A group of men came to our village and lined the girls up side by side. They looked us over carefully, from the tops of our heads to the bottoms of our feet, only accepting those they deemed perfect. The girls who passed the inspection were taken to the temple on the mountain to live in isolation, cared for by eunuchs until they were called to serve. It was an honor to be chosen and my parents were proud—as was I.

I was to be a sexual sacrifice to our sun god, Ryca. I would help our people remain under his protection and in his favor.

Six years later, the seven of us who were of age were paraded before the leaders. They did another thorough inspection, including an examination to determine our virginity. I burned with shame as they pulled my lower lips apart and touched the small opening of my womanhood. Apparently, they were satisfied with my purity and I was taken to a special area to be bathed and prepared. Unfortunately, one of the other girls was sent back to her village in a cloud of disgrace.

****

I am dressed in a simple white gown of the finest cloth, my hair left free-flowing except for the symbolic gold headband that marks me as a sacrifice. I notice my band has a ruby in the center. It signifies that I have been chosen for the head priest, the highest honor. I am to be the first to be 'sacrificed'.

I am escorted through the throngs of villagers from distant communities who have gathered to be a part of the sacred ceremony. Naturally, only men are allowed to witness the holy ritual.

I see that the high priest wears an elaborate headdress that makes him look like Ryca. The headdress is shiny gold, like the sun, and the engraved rays shoot out from the center. I am in awe of his beauty. Then I notice his robes are open, revealing his nakedness underneath. For the first time, I see the instrument of my deflowering and I freeze. His manhood is darker than the rest of his body, and large, like a fifth appendage. My joy at being chosen is now replaced with apprehension. I cannot move, so the two men escorting me take my arms and guide me towards the altar.

Once beside it, they turn me towards the crowd and the men begin to chant. It is a solemn song that beseeches Ryca to accept the sacrifice as a token of faith from his people. At the end of the chant, the escorts disrobe me and I stand naked before the assembly. Their eyes are upon me, taking in every inch of my body without shame. I read hunger in their eyes, and it makes me quiver.

I am the sacrifice.

The priest speaks behind me in a voice that booms over the crowd. "Bring her to me!" The escorts easily lift me off the ground and carry me to the stone altar. They lay me down, adjusting my position and combing out my hair so that I am perfectly displayed for our god.

The priest stands at the foot of the altar and shrugs off his robes. He is completely naked. I see his broad chest free of hair and his tanned skin glistening in the sun. He truly is the sun god, Ryca, to me.

Ryca climbs onto the altar. The two escorts each simultaneous-

ly take my legs and lift them into the air so the crowd can act as witnesses. His large hand strokes my stomach and then rests on my mound. "Are you a willing sacrifice?"

"Yes," I answer clearly. Although I am nervous, I have been groomed for this. I do not question my duty.

"Good," he grunts. He settles himself between my legs and takes his great shaft in his hand to position it against my virginal hole. I feel the warm head of his member pressing hard. He is far too large, but it does not deter him as he pushes with more force against the flesh that valiantly protects my virginity. "I want blood, Sacrifice."

I begin to…

"Hand in your books," Mr. Gallant instructed.

Brie sighed in frustration. Once again, she had spent so much time setting up the fantasy that she'd left no time for the good stuff. She raised her hand and waited to be called on. "Mr. Gallant, may I take my book home to finish?"

"I'm sorry—until the end of the course your book remains here. What is the problem?"

"I barely started detailing what happens when he takes me."

Mr. Gallant cleared his throat with an amused expression. "I am sure if a Dom is given the fantasy he will be able to navigate that part. But to be fair to you, I will read over it and hand it back during your break to complete if I deem it necessary."

Their first practicum of the night involved playing with some of the different bondage devices Mr. Gallant had mentioned in class, so that they could decide for themselves which ones they personally enjoyed. Instead of Doms, the girls were allowed to experiment with each other under the watchful eyes of their four trainers.

For the first time during their training, Brie heard Mary laugh uncontrollably as she zapped Lea with a violet wand. Lea twisted and squirmed under the electrical stimulation, but begged for more. The sound of Mary's laughter caused Brie to pause for a moment. The woman had been through so much in her life, and yet…she still had a little girl inside who had not been crushed. Mary had *had* to build walls to protect herself but, in this environment, those walls were slowly coming down.

During the break, a messenger gave Brie a note from Mr. Gallant. *"There is no need for you to write further. Enjoy the evening."*

Brie was a tad disappointed, but trusted Mr. Gallant's assessment. Just like with Rytsar, the winning Dom would have to improvise with Brie's fantasy. Maybe Doms liked it when that happened. If the roles were reversed, Brie would certainly enjoy having creative license over her sub.

She was in for a wonderful surprise when Tono joined her on stage for the second practicum. The intoxicating Dom, with those long dark bangs covering his sexy chocolate eyes, smiled at her. She quickly looked down at her feet, not wanting to hear Ms. Clark's reprimand. Brie could not quite hide her smile, though.

Tono saved her from her unwilling obedience by lifting her chin and kissing her. "Toriko, it has been far too long." He whispered in her ear, "I plan to bind you tonight and have my way with your body." She melted at his words, but stood quietly, waiting for his command.

He surprised Brie by moving behind her and wrapping his arms around her front. Then he began untying her corset ever so slowly while he breathed down her neck. She leaned her head back against his shoulder.

The corset slid off effortlessly. Then she felt his hands move to the waistband of her skirt, slide underneath and stroke her pussy through the material of her thong. He proceeded to unzip the little skirt and let it drop to the floor. He kissed his way down her back and removed her panties with his teeth. She stepped out of them, holding her breath in joyful anticipation.

Tono ran his hands up her inner thighs, lightly brushing her hairless mound before standing up and caressing her shoulders. "Do you trust me to bind you?"

"Yes, Tono," she answered without reservation.

"Before we start, I want you to present yourself to me."

Brie instantly knelt down and arched her back, pressed her chest forward, with her head down and her legs spread far apart, just as he had instructed her.

"I see you still remember my preference. That is good, toriko." His hand moved over the curve of her ass. "It's as beautiful as I remember. You may stand now."

Tono took off his shirt, showing off his trim, muscular body. He was strikingly beautiful—in a manly way. Just seeing him bare-chested left Brie panting for more. He led her to a table covered in plastic that had been brought on stage while he'd been undressing her.

He commanded her to lie down on her back and

stroked the undersides of her arms as he pulled them over her head. He secured them with nylon rope and tied her to the table. His hands then trailed down the swells of her body until he came to her ankle. He moved it into position and wrapped the rope around it several times, securing it tightly. Tono smiled at her as he took her last appendage and tied it to the table as well.

He glanced between her legs and commented, "I see the call of the rope excites you."

Brie nodded, not embarrassed that he knew how turned on she was. However, it was not just the rope that was making her hot. Tono's proximity had that effect on her.

His hands were on her again, rubbing over her stomach, her chest and between her thighs. "Tonight, I am going to turn you into art with wax."

She fidgeted nervously. "Will the hot wax hurt?"

"You tell me," he answered with a mischievous grin.

An assistant came out with a tray of burning candles in small jars and a large silver bowl. Her heart started racing when Tono picked up one of the candles.

"Close your eyes," he instructed. She obediently closed them and then heard his masculine voice next to her ear. "Enjoy."

She jumped when the hot wax made contact with her bellybutton and pooled there. Tono spread the wax out with his finger and then added more. Brie purred. The hot wax combined with his touch felt deliciously sensual...

"Open your eyes, little slave." She looked into his chocolate orbs and sighed in contentment. "I am going to cover your entire torso in wax. Lie still and let the sensations carry you."

He turned to the other girls before he began. "Not just any candle wax will do. You need one that melts at a low temperature, or you will suffer burns."

When Tono turned back to her, Brie smiled up at him. She did not jump when he poured more of the hot liquid on her stomach and it dripped down her side. The temperature reminded her of a hot, steamy shower. It was the kind of heat that was almost *too* hot, but dangerously addictive.

Her body eagerly anticipated the hot wax, but Tono surprised her. It appeared that he was going to pour more wax over her chest, but he dragged a piece of ice under the swell of her breast with his other hand. She cried out at the unexpected temperature difference.

He chuckled softly as he poured the hot liquid on her nipple. She moaned, enjoying the contrasting sensations and the ticklish feeling as the wax dribbled onto the table. It was like an erotic massage, but he kept her on her toes because he continually teased her with the cool ice.

When he'd finished covering her body in a thick layer of white wax, he took a paintbrush and began creating a simple design in black. She watched in fascination as he turned a few basic strokes into the outline of an exquisite orchid.

Tono put the paintbrush down and told her to close her eyes for a second. She nearly jumped out of her skin when he placed an ice cube on her burning clit. "First the ice, and then the fire…" He poured the hot wax on her now freezing pussy. She whimpered as the fiery liquid covered her clit and dripped slowly down her folds. "Such a nice contrast. Isn't it?" he murmured.

Brie opened her eyes to answer her handsome Dom. "It's delicious."

He snapped his fingers and the assistant returned to remove the candles and ice.

Brie looked at his work, feeling pride at being his sensuous piece of art. "Thank you, Tono."

"We are not done yet, toriko." He moved between her legs and untied them. He gently pulled her ass to the edge of the table and lifted her legs up, straightening them carefully. "You must hold this position. Do not move, or you will ruin my art."

She nodded, but gasped softly when she saw him undress. He positioned himself in between her legs and reminded her again not to move. She stifled a cry when she felt the head of his shaft press against her opening.

"No, toriko. Your Master wants to hear your pleasure."

"Yes, Tono." Brie moaned as he slowly inserted his cock into her desperate pussy. She was sorely tempted to wrap her legs around him, but his command was to keep her legs straight.

He slid himself in and then all the way back out several times, teasing her pussy with his cock. Soon Brie's legs began to shake. Tono leaned forward as he pushed deeper into her. "Point your toes and reach for the ceiling."

She followed his instructions and found it helped with the shaking.

"I'm going to ramp it up, little one." He grabbed onto her thighs and began pumping his manhood into her.

She panted as she struggled to keep her legs straight under his onslaught. "You are allowed to come, my slave, but only if you do not move." One of his hands moved to her clit and began flicking it vigorously.

By then, Brie's stomach muscles were aching from her efforts to keep her legs straight, but it added to the whole experience and she felt her inner muscles start to contract. Her body released all of the pent-up desire she had built up during the scene. Her passionate moans filled the small auditorium. His masculine grunts soon followed as he pumped his seed into her.

Tears of effort fell from her eyes. "I can't last much longer…" she whimpered.

"A little longer is all I ask," he answered, as he pulled away from her and petted her sex. "This is the first time I've had the chance to enjoy your bare mound, toriko. It is a lovely flower, especially after just being taken." He pushed her farther onto the table and took her legs, slowly bending them and placing them back down so she could rest.

"You look beautiful, my little slave. It is a shame that I must release you from the wax."

The assistant returned with a large knife. Brie's eyes widened when Tono brought it up to her chest. He deftly unsealed the edges of the wax and put the knife down. Then he peeled it off in one large piece, leaving the art perfectly intact. "This is for you, in exchange for the panties I confiscated on our first day," he said with a wicked little smirk.

He helped her off the table, ordering her to stand. Then he picked up the knife again. She couldn't help cringing when he slid it over her skin. "You must remain still as I remove all the pieces, little one."

Her trust in him was so deep that she did not resist the feel of the sharp blade caressing her skin; she gave in to it. It felt dangerously delicious in the hands of a master.

Just before he finished, Tono moved his lips to her ear and whispered, "I *will* win the auction this week."

With all her heart, Brie hoped that he would.

Pushing Limits

Brie got a taste of her boundaries the next night during her second practicum. A young, Asian Domme joined her up on the stage with a ball gag in her hand. Brie stared at it warily. Just seeing the red ball made her sick to her stomach.

"Turn, pet," the petite woman commanded when Brie had knelt before her.

Brie hesitantly turned and forced herself not to close her eyes—her normal mode of defense when something was difficult.

"Open."

Brie opened her lips, but not wide enough. Her Domme commanded her to open wider in order to fit the ball gag in her mouth. It stretched Brie's jaw uncomfortably and a cold chill traveled down her spine.

The Asian Domme fastened the gag and commanded that she stand up. Brie shuddered, hating the ball gag with even greater passion when she felt drool spill from her mouth. There was nothing sexy about it.

"Miss Bennett," Sir called out. She turned to him,

trying not to look as miserable as she felt. "Do you want the gag removed?"

It would be another failure if she said yes, and she didn't want to fail again. However, she was sorely tempted to remove the hated device.

From the audience, she heard Mary say, "It's what your Domme wants."

Her words flooded through Brie. *Yes, this is what my Mistress wants.* To deny such a basic thing would take away from the scene her Mistress had created. Brie realized her discomfort was not severe enough to remove the ball gag and looked back at Sir, shaking her head.

He reminded her, "If at any time you wish to change your mind, snap your fingers."

She bowed to him in answer and then turned to her Domme. She would ignore the drooling and the ache of her jaw if it brought her Mistress pleasure.

"Obedience is always rewarded," her Domme stated. "I have a surprise for you, pet. But first you must be properly prepared."

She directed Brie to an interesting chair. It was reminiscent of a folding beach chair because of its adjustability, although this version was far sturdier. First, she bound Brie's wrists to the arms of the chair with rope. Then the tiny Domme bent Brie's right leg and pushed it up and to the side. She began winding the rope around Brie's ankle, binding her in that position. She did the same to Brie's left leg, leaving her legs spread and her bare pussy splayed out and exposed.

Her Domme asked her to get out of the restraints.

Brie struggled but could not move. A thrill of helplessness coursed through her. Her Domme could do whatever she wanted now, and Brie would be powerless to stop it.

Her thin lips curved into a smile. "I think you are ready for my surprise, pet."

A man entered the stage. The ball in her mouth muffled Brie's gasp. The submissive male model from the week before was approaching her. He wore black latex pants with a hole in the crotch. His mighty shaft was exposed and firm. Her eyes widened as the branch of a cock made its way over to her pussy.

"My submissive mentioned seeing you in Mr. Gallant's class. He's been an exceptionally good boy this week, so I have decided to reward him."

Brie's pussy contracted in pleasure and a bit of trepidation. His was the most massive cock she had ever seen. *Can I even take it?*

The Domme adjusted the back of the chair to a lower angle. She began to caress Brie's breasts as the sub moved between Brie's legs. "You will need to relax, pet. I want to see his entire shaft disappear inside your submissive cunt."

Brie concentrated on the feeling of her Domme playing with her nipples, hoping the release of oxytocin would help her body receive the gift of the submissive's giant cock. It wasn't lost on Brie that this scene was deliciously reminiscent of her virgin sacrifice fantasy, and it totally turned her on. *I am the sacrifice!*

Her Domme commanded the male sub, "Rub your cock on her pussy, Boa. Get that little cunt used to your girth and juicy for your invasion."

Boa? Well, he does have a huge snake of a cock…

Brie felt him rub the enormous head of his shaft against her tiny clit. If she hadn't wanted this, it might have been intimidating. As it was, she was extremely curious how he would feel slipping into her moist recess. Boa spent time teasing her with his shaft, rubbing it sideways over her little nub, and then up and down between her wet outer lips. There was just so incredibly much of him!

"Take her now," the Domme commanded.

Brie moaned against the ball in her mouth as Boa positioned the head of his cock against her small opening and started to push. She was shocked at the huge circumference now that he was trying to power his way in. He grabbed her hips and thrust harder. It didn't seem possible that he could penetrate her small opening until he pushed through the resistance and forced the head of his enormous shaft inside her.

Brie grunted from the deep ache it caused. It took everything in her to accept his endowment. His proportions challenged her body in ways she had never experienced before—and this had only just begun.

"That's a good start," her Domme purred, playing with Brie's nipples. "Take his cock into your little cunt."

Boa kept thrusting, but it seemed her body couldn't take any more. He began caressing her bare pussy. "Open up to me," he growled lustfully.

"Give yourself to him, pet." Her Domme's warm lips fell on Brie's left nipple, and she began sucking on it as her other hand rolled Brie's right nipple between her delicate fingers.

Brie visualized her inner walls lengthening to accommodate Boa's size. She moaned when he pushed in another inch.

"That's it, pet. That's it…" the Domme cooed.

The thrusting continued as Boa inched his massive cock into her willing depths. Her Domme lifted Brie's head up and commanded her to look. "See how deep inside he is, pet? Look how stretched your lips are. It doesn't seem as if you can take more, does it? But you can."

Brie was amazed to see her body taking his huge shaft, which was glistening with her wetness. Only a fourth of him remained unclaimed, but there was no way she could take more. *No way…*

"Remain still," the Domme ordered her male sub. He instantly stopped his movements and waited for her next command.

Her Mistress adjusted the chair again so that Brie was lying flat. She then poured oil onto Brie's chest and began massaging her breasts expertly. It was sensual and intimate, made that much more tantalizing because of the oversized cock planted inside her.

The Domme leaned towards her ear. "I am going to have Boa thrust the rest of the way in now. Your body is primed and ready. I get so hot watching this part."

She looked up at her sub. "Do it."

Without hesitation, Boa grabbed Brie's waist and thrust. She screamed in pleasure and pain against the ball gag as he pushed his shaft to the hilt. Her body became completely, utterly filled.

Boa stopped again and caressed her thighs. "So beautiful," he commented.

"Yes, she is. Such a lovely cunt." Her Domme reached down and played with Brie's clit. "Concentrate on the large cock inside you and come for me."

Brie closed her eyes and reveled in the fact that Boa's massive shaft was deep inside her now. It didn't take long for her pussy to begin contracting in pleasure, but her orgasm felt different. Her inner muscles were so stretched that they barely squeezed against his sizable girth.

"There will be plenty more before he is done," the tiny Domme informed Brie as she stood up and walked over to Boa. Her hands lightly danced over his stomach and down to his groin. She touched the base of his cock where it met the rim of Brie's lips.

"You want to fuck her now, don't you?"

He nodded.

"It is my pleasure to give you this treat, Boa. I *always* reward obedience." Her hands moved from his groin and up to his chest. She tweaked his nipples playfully and then turned his head, kissing him on the lips.

"I am yours, Mistress," he said with a low growl.

Her fingers trailed over his lips. "Yes, and you proved it this week." The Domme moved back over to Brie. Her hands were like magic as she massaged Brie's aching breasts. "And you shall be rewarded as well, pet, for wearing the gag I required. Had you resisted my desire, you would have been fucked with a dildo instead." She wiped the drool from Brie's mouth. "And that would not have been nearly as fun, now, would it?"

Brie shook her head.

Her Domme positioned her face next to Brie's cheek with her arms on either side of her breasts, stroking, caressing and teasing her nipples. "Are you ready?"

Brie's body tensed in anticipation as she nodded.

"Good," the Domme purred seductively. She looked up at Boa and smiled. "Fuck her."

He pulled nearly all the way out and then slammed himself back in. Brie's muffled cries filled the auditorium as he pumped his giant dick inside her.

"Faster, Boa. Fuck her deep!" her Domme demanded. The Asian Domme groaned in unison with Boa as if the two of them were connected, as if they were both fucking Brie together.

The frenzied thrusts of his gargantuan cock took Brie to another plane of existence. Her eyes rolled back in her head as she became *one* with the cock. It possessed her completely. She gave in to the claiming of her body and started to float. Pleasant electrical sparks radiated from her groin in a rhythmic pattern. In her dreamy state, it took several moments to realize that she was having one long, continuous orgasm. She whimpered in pleasure.

"She likes it, Boa, just like we knew she would."

He only grunted in response as he stroked Brie with his colossal shaft over and over again.

Finally, she heard her Domme cry out, "Now!"

Boa grasped Brie's shoulders and sank his rigid staff as deep as her body could take. She shook her head from side to side as his shaft exploded with a massive release of come. She screamed around the rubber ball, the aching pleasure clouding all other sensations. Her body responded by clamping down on his immense cock with one final orgasmic contraction.

Brie vaguely felt the bonds loosen, and then her Domme pushed the chair back into a sitting position. With gentle hands, she cleaned between Brie's legs with a wet cloth. "Now your cunt knows the feeling of possession." She then reached around Brie's head and undid the ball gag. She pulled the ball away, and a long string of saliva followed. The Domme wiped that away as well. She helped Brie up from the chair.

Brie stood before the panel, woozy but quite satiated.

Sir asked, "How would you rate the scene, Miss Bennett?"

She stood there with a huge smile. No words formed, so she just nodded.

"It was good for you, then?"

She continued to nod slowly.

Marquis Gray asked, "Miss Bennett, why did you resist the ball gag?"

His question actually caused her to think, so she struggled out of her pleasant stupor to reply. "It's…uncomfortable."

"But how does a ball gag make you *feel*, Miss Bennett?" he pressed.

"What do you mean, Marquis Gray?" She was frustrated, knowing he wanted some other answer. "It hurts my jaw, and I don't care for all the drooling."

She noticed him frown, although the expression did not reach down to his mouth. He wrote something in his notes, and it made Brie squirm to see it. She seemed to be missing something vital.

Brie came face-to-face with her boundary the next day—
Marquis Gray made sure of that. A bare-chested Dom
came onto the stage, dressed only in black leather pants.
"Bow at my feet, slut."

Brie's eyes narrowed. She hesitated; no one had
called her a slut before and it rubbed her the wrong way.

"Now," he commanded.

She knelt down at his feet reluctantly. When a table
was set beside her, Brie stealthily peeked. What she saw
made her skin crawl. There was a butt plug with a pig's
tail, a ball gag, collar and leash, and a violet wand.

"Undress and present yourself to me."

As she undressed, Brie looked out to the seats. Mary
was sitting on the edge of her chair, obviously aroused
by the scenario about to play out. It made sense—Mary
enjoyed this kind of scene. Brie took a deep breath and
got on all fours, presenting herself sexually to her Dom.

"What a nasty cunt you are," he snarled lustfully,
slapping her on the ass. "You know what I do with dirty
sluts like you?" He fisted her hair and pulled back her
head sharply so that she was forced to look at him. "I
treat them like the dirty pig sluts they are." He let her go
and walked over to the table. He picked up the collar
first.

"Come here, little piggy."

When she started to stand, he commanded, "On all

fours, like the horny pig you are."

Brie tried to crawl on the floor towards him seductively, but she wasn't feeling it—not in the least. The Dom fastened the heavy leather collar over Sir's. It felt *so* wrong. Then he attached the leash and yanked on it. "Come."

He led her around the stage. Brie kept her eyes cast downward, struggling to please him as she crawled like an animal. He was not satisfied and remarked, "I think I know what the problem is. You don't feel like a slutty little pig yet." He lubed the butt plug with the curly pig's tail, and then picked up the gag.

Brie imagined herself down on all fours with the hated ball gag in her mouth, saliva dripping from her lips, while her Dom called out, "piggy, piggy" as he shoved that horrible pig's tail plug into her ass. It was too much and she began shaking her head violently.

My Master wants this… She almost convinced herself, but the moment he touched her ass with the plug, something snapped inside her. She screamed at the top of her lungs, "Red, red, red!"

The Dom immediately took the toy away. She scrambled to her feet and faced the panel. Another failure, but Brie had *had* to end the scene—being treated like a pig would have crushed her. She removed the unwanted collar and let it drop to the stage floor.

Marquis Gray was the first to address her. "Why was this difficult for you, Miss Bennett?"

"I couldn't let him do that to me."

"How would the butt plug have hurt you? You've taken them before."

"I…" She shook her head as she fought for the right words to express her disdain. "That thing is vile." She looked at Marquis Gray, struggling against the emotions boiling inside her. "It made me feel…*bad.*"

"Similar to the ball gag?" he asked.

She nodded her head.

"And relieving yourself in front of Rytsar Durov?"

Brie shook her head at first, but then realized he was right. "Not to the same degree, but yes."

Sir cleared his throat. She looked at him sadly, hoping he understood.

"In one word, how did those things make you feel, Miss Bennett?"

She felt the tears coming and whispered, "Humiliated…"

"Yes."

Brie looked at Sir through watery eyes. "Is it something required of a sub, Sir?"

His expression softened. "No, Miss Bennett. However, it is vital that you tell your Doms it is a trigger for you."

She nodded and felt a surge of relief when he smiled reassuringly. "This was an important lesson for you. Take time to process it. Some submissives find there is considerable freedom in acting out scenes of humiliation. Others need to feel treasured and cannot find comfort in such an experience. The decision is yours."

"Thank you, Sir." She turned back to Marquis Gray. "Thank you, Marquis."

The ghostly trainer nodded his head. "Miss Bennett, I plan to help you with another hurdle tomorrow. Are you prepared for a real challenge?"

His intense stare sent a shiver of unease and excitement through her. "Yes, Master."

A hint of a smile played across his eyes and lips at her use of that title.

She bowed to the panel and left the stage, humbled by the encounter. There was no feeling of contentment that normally followed a scene, and she felt some sympathy for the Dom as he walked off the stage with his collection of 'toys'. However, Brie was grateful for the experience. Just as Sir had promised, she was discovering fears and desires she had never known existed.

Marquis Expands Her Power

Brie had only experienced one session with Marquis Gray. His lesson had been the most challenging for her because of his expertise—whipping. She shivered under her covers when she woke up the next morning, curious about how he would test her this session. The last time he had used a flogger. What would tonight bring?

Unfortunately, Brie was late to the Training Center because her coworker, Jeff, had shown up a half-hour late to the tobacco shop. She had been the only employee working that day, so she'd been forced to wait. She made up time by throwing on her uniform and driving way too fast, but she would still be fifteen minutes late to her first class. It made Brie ill to think of entering Mr. Gallant's classroom after his lesson had started.

She ran as fast as she could in her six-inch heels and was relieved that Blue Eyes was still at the door, ready to hold it open for her. He gave her a wink. "You made it."

"Thanks," she replied, panting heavily as she rushed through the door.

He called after her, "You might want to check those hose."

Brie looked down and saw that the seam was twisted around her leg. She groaned, but made a detour to the bathroom to remedy the problem. She took off her shoes and adjusted the hose, making sure the seam made a tantalizing trail up her leg. Then she checked the mirror and smoothed out her hair. She took several deep calming breaths and smiled. *Yes, I am late, but there is no reason to enter class like a raving lunatic.*

With forced ease, she glided into Mr. Gallant's class and sat down. He looked up at her with a scowl but did not interrupt his lesson. "…other themes using bondage are interrogations, rape fantasies and sexual torture. Depending on the individuals, these can be fairly tame to quite intense. Remember to establish a nonverbal safety gesture if gags are to be used. Nothing is worse for a Dom than to discover he has gone past his sub's level of endurance *after* the session has ended. Trust me, it is hard on both parties and should be avoided at all costs."

Brie's mind drifted in and out of his lesson as she worried what he was going to say to her afterwards. "Miss Bennett?"

She snapped her head up and stammered, "Yes, Mr. Gallant."

He repeated the question, obviously annoyed. "For your next auction, you must decide if you want your fantasy fulfilled or your Dom's."

That was easy. After her session with Boa, she'd felt she *had* lived out her fantasy. What she truly desired was to live out Tono's. Brie knew she was taking a risk that he might not win her, but she was confident in her decision. "I will fulfill my Dom's, Mr. Gallant."

"Fine." He turned away abruptly, and asked Mary the same question. Brie didn't like having Mr. Gallant unhappy with her. She understood the importance of being punctual, but surely he realized she had responsibilities outside this Center. Would he understand or would she be punished? She gave a nervous sigh when he dismissed the class and called her name.

"Miss Bennett, I need to speak with you."

Lea gave her a sympathetic look as she walked past. Even though the man was tiny in stature, he had the commanding authority of a true Dominant. It was torture displeasing him.

"You know being late is considered a sign of disrespect."

Brie couldn't even look him in the eye. "I know, Mr. Gallant. And I *do* respect you tremendously."

"Look at me and tell me why you were late today."

Words spewed from her mouth in a torrent. "It was all that damn Jeff's fault! That lazy ass never does his job and is always late to work. Normally it isn't a problem for me, but my boss wasn't there today. I was the only one in the shop. You have to understand that I *had* to wait for the bastard because I couldn't leave the shop unattended. Mr. Gallant, I would never be late if I could help it."

She was surprised by the severe look he gave her. "I can appreciate your predicament, but I must say I am offended by your words. I should never hear curse words come from your lips unless I ask for them, and you should *not* belittle others as a sub. It would have sufficed to say, 'Mr. Gallant, my coworker was late, and I was the only one in the shop today.'"

Brie burned with shame. "Yes, that sounds much better."

"I want you to speak to your boss and explain that your coworker made you late to a previous engagement. You cannot control your coworker, but you can inform your boss of the problem and hope it prevents such occurrences in the future."

She breathed a huge sigh of relief. "Thank you, Mr. Gallant. I was afraid you would punish me for being late."

"Miss Bennett, we do not practice random punishments at this school. You can always expect fair treatment if you are open and honest."

She was so thankful that she blurted, "I just want to hug you right now!"

He replied sternly, "That would be inappropriate." Brie thought she saw just the slightest glimmer in his eye. She genuinely liked her teacher, and wondered again what it would be like to be under his control as his submissive. "That is all. You may join the others."

With the utmost respect, she bowed to him. "Thank you, Teacher."

She was smiling to herself when she left the classroom. Brie really loved this school because she felt respected as an individual. Best of all, she was learning to better herself and knew it would have a positive influence on her life outside these walls.

She walked to their regular classroom but found no

one there. She hurried down the hall towards the auditorium, but was stopped by an assistant. "Your practicum has been moved to room nine."

Brie thanked him and wasted no time making her way to the new classroom. It sucked that she was going to be late to another session. She stopped herself and took a couple of deep breaths before opening the door and entering. What she saw caused her stomach to roll. The room was wall-to-wall mirrors except for the wall opposite the door, which was covered in different punishment tools, including whips, paddles and harsh-looking metal devices.

As disconcerting as that was, however, the sight of Marquis Gray standing next to a bench, waiting for her with a cane in his hand, made her stop in her tracks.

"Miss Bennett, join Marquis Gray," Sir said smoothly.

Marquis Gray motioned with his hand. "Come to me, pearl. We will confront your fear of the cane together."

She gazed into his dark eyes, drawn in by his confidence despite her misgivings. "Yes, Master."

A genuine smile spread across his face. "I appreciate your trust, pearl. I know you will find this rewarding."

The bench reminded her of a workout bench in that it was long and thin. The only real difference was that it was taller and had leather cuffs attached.

"I shall undress you, but you must hold this in your mouth while I do." He placed the thin stick between her teeth. "This is your rattan, pearl. I bought it especially for you. It will be our instrument of pleasure tonight," he growled in a low, sensual tone.

She clamped down on it as Marquis Gray slowly undressed her, lightly caressing her skin as he did so. The fear mounting inside her only added to the sensual feel of his undressing. "Remember to breathe normally," he reminded her when he noticed Brie gasping in short, shallow breaths. She nodded and took a deeper breath.

He asked her to bend over and hold on to the bench while he secured her wrists in cuffs. "This is the classic English position. You need to keep your back straight throughout the session," he said as he repositioned her. "Spread those legs farther. I want your pussy open and visible." He stepped back and took a long look before returning to her. "You are not allowed to move from this position."

A shiver traveled through her whole body when Marquis Gray took the rod from her mouth and asked, "Are you ready, pearl?"

She only hesitated for a second. The truth was, she wanted to know how it would feel under Marquis' expert hand, and if she would be able to take it. "Yes, Master."

"No matter how tempted you are to move, you must remain still," he warned her. "Trust me to create the sensations I desire, even if your body initially wants to resist it."

"I will try, Master."

"No! You will *not* move," he insisted.

Properly chastised, she replied, "Yes, Master."

He leaned over and told her confidently, "When I've finished with you tonight, you will know without question whether your fear of the cane was unfounded.

Whatever the outcome, I guarantee you will have greater insight into your real desires."

Brie's loins tightened in anticipation when he stepped away. She immediately looked at their reflection in the mirror and saw him take a stance behind her with his knees slightly bent. He pulled his arm back for the first swing.

She swallowed hard and inadvertently closed her eyes as she readied herself for the first contact, but it did not come. She took a quick peek and saw that he had turned towards the other girls. "As with flogging, you do not want a novice using you for practice. A Dom must research and practice for many hours before he ever touches another person with a cane."

Brie wondered if he was playing with her by delaying the first swing. If so, it was wickedly cruel. He caressed her ass with the rod as he continued to speak. "Also, I suggest asking your Dom if he has ever been caned. My personal opinion is that you cannot know the sensations you are creating unless you have experienced them yourself." He gently rapped her bottom, teasing her with the instrument. "A Dom opposed to such an education exposes his lack of wisdom."

He continued to caress and tap Brie's round buttocks as he spoke. "I don't recommend caning as punishment. It is far too effective as a sexual tool to relegate it to a lowly reprimand implement." He ran the cane up and down her thighs before striking her on the ass. "Do you see how wet it makes her?"

Brie flushed, embarrassed that her body was giving her away. She didn't want Mary and Lea to know how excited she was. This wasn't even something she'd wanted. The idea of caning had always frightened her, and yet here she was, willingly bent over and ready to receive her first session with the cane.

"First, I will warm up your sweet little ass, pearl. This will feel pleasing." She watched in the mirror as he stroked her with a circular motion. The cane bounced lightly off her buttocks with a soft thud. It was totally pleasant, even relaxing. He alternated it with a gentle rapping. When her skin was pleasantly warm, he asked, "Color?"

"Green, Master."

He asked the other students, "Why do I warm up before I begin?"

Lea raised her hand. She licked her lips before answering Marquis, clearly turned on by Brie's imminent caning. "The cane is less likely to do damage if the skin is prepared."

"Very good." He turned his attention back on Brie. "Pearl, it is time to increase your pleasure." He swung the cane and it landed squarely on both buttocks at once. She cried out. The sting was intense and brought tears to her eyes, but quickly dissipated outward from deep within her body.

"Color?"

"Yellow," she gasped.

"Don't become rigid, pearl." He patted her ass cheeks lightly. "Relax and let the cane vibrate through you. Don't stop it by tensing your muscles and it will feel better."

Brie turned her head to watch in the mirror. He took

another swing, and she witnessed the strike as she felt it. Her ass jiggled alluringly upon impact and she let out another yelp. The sting gripped her groin like a vice and then the heat dissipated through her whole body. This time she moaned afterwards. Although the sting took her breath away, the feeling it created after was delicious.

"Color, pearl."

"Yell…green."

He caressed her pink ass and proclaimed, "Now you will take five strokes. Don't move or I will not hit where I intend."

She bit her lip, wondering if she could survive five in a row.

Raising the cane a bit higher, he gave quick, moderate strokes. The small room was filled with the slapping sounds of impact. Each stroke was slightly higher than the last so that he never hit the same area twice. The release was much more intense after five rapid strokes, and Brie whimpered, shuddering at the lusty fire bursting inside her.

"You took that well, pearl. Now we will do it from the other side."

When he moved to the left side and raised the cane, she cried out, "Not yet!"

"Five more." With rapid movements, he struck her five times, covering the areas in between her first marks. She begged him to stop just before the last stroke. He didn't hesitate, giving the last one with the same force. This time, he left the cane pressed against her skin. It made the sting linger, but the engulfing tidal wave of heat that burst from inside caused her knees to buckle and her pussy to pulse.

"You are close, aren't you?" Marquis Gray growled.

Brie nodded, afraid he would cane her again but desperately wanting the burst of fire to send her over the edge.

"I will not deny you the pleasure this time. I want your body to remember and drip in anticipation whenever you see the cane." Brie moaned in response, expecting a final stroke. Instead, he placed the cane against her lips. "Hold this, pearl." She opened her mouth and held her cane, while he unbuckled her wrists.

He moved her over to the wooden Saint Andrew's cross. The large X-shaped frame sported metal cuffs. He quickly bound her facing towards him. Her buttocks rested against the wood, aching from the contact. Brie's arms and legs were bound far apart, fully exposing her body to his desire.

"This time I want you to close your eyes. You won't know where the strike is coming from because I want you to focus on the sensation it evokes." He took the cane from her mouth and asked, "Color?"

"Green, Master."

"Close your eyes then, my courageous pearl." As soon as she did, he began lightly caressing her breasts with the cane. He moved lower and caressed her hips before turning his attention to her inner thighs. He slid the tip of the cane between her moist lips and gently stroked her clit. Brie gasped, her inner muscles contracting from the contact. She was so close she was on the verge of exploding.

She felt him step back, and she tensed again. "No,

pearl, relax. Breathe out."

As soon as she let the breath out, she felt a quick tap on the top of her right nipple. The vibration shot down to her groin. Her body began pulsating again. When he tapped the left one, it started a whole chain reaction. Her body shook as the massive orgasm took over. She did not hold back her voice, and let out a cry of passion.

When the last contraction ebbed, she felt a rap just above her clit. She whimpered in pleasure as a smaller orgasm washed over her. Before it had ended, Marquis' lips were on hers. He pressed his body against her and she felt his rigid cock straining in his pants. She opened her eyes and looked into his dark, lust-filled gaze.

"Now it is your turn to please me."

"Yes, Master," she panted, longing to share her pleasure with him.

He pressed his shaft against her as he undid the metal cuffs. Once she was free, he lifted her up and carried her back to the bench, then told her to lean against it, facing away from him. He spread her legs apart. She'd expected he would plow right in, but he bent down and lightly kissed her smarting ass. "So beautiful when it's red like this. A testament to your level of trust, pearl."

He removed his clothes and stood behind her. In the mirror, she could see his ghostly white skin. Marquis Gray had a thin frame, although his shoulder and chest muscles were defined. What stood out was the dark pubic hair that framed his unusual cock. His shaft was long and curved upwards.

She felt butterflies when he moved between her legs. Brie trembled as he slowly penetrated her moist depths with his unusual shaft. His deep sigh sent a wave of electrical current through her. They were both still riding the high of the scene, and it added to their level of connection now. His curved shaft repeatedly stroked the roof of her vagina, making it impossible for her to think.

He pulled away and brought back a leather strap, placing it under her belly and then gathering it in his hands. He parted her moist pussy lips and entered her again, and both of them groaned in satisfaction. Marquis Gray lifted her waist using the strap, causing a delightful pressure in her groin as he thrust. It added a completely new level of pleasure. "Too good…" she whimpered.

He leaned towards her, pushing himself in deep. "I'm going to come now. Feel the strength of my climax, pearl. It is for you." He pulled on the leather strap as he gave her long, deep strokes. They were unhurried, giving her the chance to appreciate all of the sensuous feelings his cock was generating.

A deep groan rumbled from his throat and she felt his manhood pulse powerfully inside her. It triggered a third wave of heat and her body came around his shaft, bathing him with her juices.

When he pulled out, he commanded that she turn around to face him. She looked up with glazed eyes, still enjoying the incredible high. "Hold onto me," he ordered. Marquis Gray held out his arm, and she grabbed onto it. He led her to a small door in a corner of the room. An assistant was already there, holding it open.

Marquis Gray guided her through it. The tiny room reminded her of the one in the auditorium. It had a small bed and a table with several candles already lit. When the assistant shut the door and left, they were suddenly shrouded in darkness except for the warm light of the flames.

They lay on the bed together, the same as they had the last time. He spooned against her, pulling Brie against his naked body. He didn't speak. It left her free to be hypnotized by the candle flames as they danced on the wicks. Soon, however, she began shivering.

"You did well today," he said, nuzzling her ear.

She snuggled deeper into him, her ass burning from the contact. "You are a master of the cane, Marquis Gray."

"I knew you would enjoy it, pearl. I have been waiting patiently to show you."

She turned her head towards him. "How could you know I would like it when I stated from the beginning that it frightened me?"

His fingers caressed her cheek. "Your desire called to me."

Another shiver racked her body, but she wasn't sure if it was solely due to coming down from the natural high. She rolled over so that she was facing him. Brie traced the outline of his thin lips. Marquis Gray had always been so intimidating and fearsome, but there was so much more to the man. "How did you know I struggled with humiliation? You knew it early on and warned me."

"You have a strong spirit. I am not surprised that humiliation is not arousing for you. However, I must ask. Would you want a Dom who will never humiliate you, or would you prefer a man who will challenge you in that area from time to time? Some women find that realization of being nothing acutely liberating."

Brie put her hand on his slim but defined chest. She caressed his smooth muscles absently as she struggled with the question. Finally, she knew her answer and looked into those cavernous eyes of his. "I would want the man who would challenge me to grow."

A smile played on his lips. "I suspected as much." He pulled her to him and said no more.

They lay together in the dark until her trembling ceased. Before they left the sanctuary of the room, he lifted her chin. "You no longer have fear of the cane, pearl. You are free."

That knowledge made Brie feel powerful. She grew determined then that fear of the unknown would no longer control her. She whispered, "Thank you, Master," as she returned his long, lingering kiss.

Auction: The Art of Kinbaku

As Brie readied herself for the auction, she kept staring at the wax mold Tono had made for her. She'd purchased a shadow box and now had the artistic piece hanging in her bedroom. The fact that he could turn such simple strokes into a beautiful flower had truly impressed her.

She was confident he would be the winning Dom for this auction so she took extra time with her makeup, giving it a more Asian flair. "I'm all yours, Tono…" she announced, grabbing her purse and heading out of her apartment door.

When Brie got to the school, she immediately noticed there was something wrong with Mary. Lea was trying to put her arm around Mary's shoulders, but Mary shook her off. It seemed Blonde Nemesis was back, as she escaped to the other side of the room.

"What's up with her?" Brie asked quietly.

"Her period came a little early."

Brie looked at her with profound sympathy. *How awful to start on Auction Day.* "What's going to happen?"

"Ms. Clark said it isn't a problem, but they'll announce it when they introduce her on stage."

"Damn… That's so embarrassing."

"Yeah."

Brie went to the array of snack foods that had been set up for them and grabbed a piece of chocolate. She walked over to Mary and watched her body stiffen as she approached. "Hey."

Mary glared at her.

"I bring a peace offering," Brie said, holding out the chocolate treat.

Mary growled under her breath, but took it and popped the chocolate in her mouth.

"Hold your head up. You have so much more to offer than just your pussy."

Mary actually cracked a smile. "Thanks."

"Hey, it's the least I could do. You really helped me this week when my Domme wanted me to wear the ball gag."

"Yeah, I regret that. Had I known you would miss out on Boa if you hadn't worn it, I would have kept my mouth shut."

Brie looked at her in shock. "Really?"

"Hell, yeah! I wanted Boa all to myself."

Brie pushed her on the shoulder and grinned. "Just so you know, he was *mighty* fine."

"Bitch."

Brie laughed, but shut right up when Ms. Clark walked in and told them it was time to line up. Mary was the first called onto the stage. Brie held her breath when the bidding started, worried that Mary would suffer another mortifying auction. The bidding started off slowly after the announcer had mentioned her feminine condition, but Brie finally heard, "Going once… Going twice… Sold to Master Cox for five hundred dollars."

Lea was next on stage. After a flurry of bidding, she was handed over to a Dom called Torres for six hundred. It appeared that as their training advanced, so did their bids.

When the announcer called her name, Brie hesitated. She had not heard Tono's voice once during the auction. She walked onto the stage with her gaze glued to the floor for Ms. Clark's benefit.

"Miss Bennett is twenty-two with a bachelor's degree in filmmaking outside these walls. Her trainers describe her as unique and pliable."

Brie felt a rush of heat settle on her cheeks. Such positive praise from the trainers was unexpected.

When the bidding began, Tono's warm voice filled the large room and she had to squelch the urge to smile by pinching herself. Several other Doms challenged his bid, and Brie felt a brush of panic at the prospect of Tono being outbid again.

"Going once… Going twice… Sold to Tono Nosaka for nine hundred dollars."

It took everything in Brie not to squeal with joy. She was Tono's for the entire day!

Her whole body flushed when he walked up and took her hand. "Come with me, toriko." She walked beside him, giddy with excitement.

Sir concluded the auction, but Tono did not move. After the room had cleared out, he approached the panel of trainers. "I am requesting to keep Miss Bennett longer than normal. I plan to do a full shoot and do not want to feel rushed. I understand the importance of the debriefing, but I promise to discuss the session afterwards, just as she would with all of you."

"This is highly unusual, Tono Nosaka," Ms. Clark complained.

Sir replied, "You do realize that the debriefing includes the other students. She will miss out on that."

"I do understand, Headmaster Davis," Tono answered respectfully. "However, I believe that Miss Bennett will benefit from a full session, given her interest in bondage."

Master Coen spoke up, "I agree. It would be a beneficial experience for our student."

"Mr. Nosaka, why would you need more than eight hours for a shoot?" Sir asked skeptically.

Tono tilted his head. "Obviously, you are not familiar with the rituals I practice both before and after a session."

Marquis Gray looked at Brie with eyes she could not read. "Before we discuss this further, we need to know if Miss Bennett is willing to do a shoot with you."

Tono turned to her, gracing Brie with his devastating chocolate gaze. "Toriko, would you allow me to photograph our session as I expose you to the art of Kinbaku?"

Brie couldn't hide her excitement when she answered, "Yes, Tono. I would like that very much."

Ms. Clark added her two cents. "Since this is a unique opportunity for Miss Bennett, I believe it merits missing one night's debriefing."

"I concur," Marquis said quietly.

Sir stared at Tono without speaking. An uncomfortable span of time passed before he stated, "You have permission to keep her until midnight, when class officially ends."

Tono bowed to Sir and guided Brie towards the elevator. His touch was soothing and electric at the same time. She found it difficult not to stare at him like a puppy dog.

It turned out that Tono drove a sleek, silver Nissan. He opened the door for her, but didn't let her enter the car. "Kiss me, toriko."

She tiptoed and pressed her lips against his. Tono's arms enfolded her as they kissed. The chemistry between them was its own living organism, a third party wrapping itself around the two. When he pulled away, she had to catch her breath.

"While you are with me today, you have permission to look me in the eye. In fact, I would prefer it, little slave." His hand grazed her cheek.

He motioned her inside his sports car and insisted she buckle up. She soon found out why when he took off. Tono liked speed, and his car was made to break the law. She squeaked several times during the drive, making him chuckle. It was obvious he was enjoying giving her an adrenaline rush of a different kind.

His tiny, unassuming home was in an older part of LA. Whereas his car was flashy and screamed success, his home was humble. The front was a simple rock garden. Inside, Brie was surprised to see it was mostly open with only a few walls, much like a studio apartment. The floors were a dark wood and the furniture sparse. His home radiated peace and tranquility. She was decidedly impressed.

A door opened from the backyard, and a beautiful Asian girl entered. She bowed to Tono. "It is ready, Master."

"Thank you, Akira. You may wait in the bedroom."

She bowed low to him, and then to Brie. Her walk was graceful as she took small steps towards the door to the far left. When Akira had quietly closed the door behind her, Brie tried to keep the jealousy out of her voice. "Is she your sub, Tono?"

He shook his head in amusement. "No, toriko. She is my assistant. She helps me with the shoots."

"Why does she call you Master?"

"Out of respect. In certain circles, I'm considered a master of the rope." His humble smile melted her heart. "It is actually the reason I was absent at the auction last week. I had a live show in New York. Normally, I don't leave California, but I wanted enough disposable income to make sure I won your auction this week. I refused to be outbid again."

Brie blushed, remembering her first auction when the Russian Dom, Rytsar, had outbid Tono. Knowing that the man before her was a renowned artist was disconcerting. "I didn't realize you were famous, Tono."

He chuckled and gathered her into his arms. "I am not famous, little slave. People simply enjoy the art, and others want to learn the technique."

Something told her that he was being overly modest,

but she accepted his answer. He pointed to a short, red kimono artfully hanging on the wall. "That is for you to wear for the shoot, toriko. You may join Akira in the bedroom. She will help you dress, and then I want you to meet me out back."

He kissed her on the forehead and left.

Brie lifted the gorgeous kimono and traced the gold thread accents with her fingers. The soft feel of the silk thrilled her. She'd never worn anything this beautiful before.

She carried it into the bedroom and spent the next half-hour being primped by Akira. She wore no clothes underneath the silken kimono. Although her makeup was simple, Akira applied a deep red lipstick and redid her eyeliner. She spent most of her time creating an elegant updo for Brie, complete with decorative chop-sticks. When Brie looked in the mirror, she saw a model staring back at her.

"Wow, Akira. You are a magician."

The woman twittered softly. "Not so, Miss Bennett. It is easy to work with natural beauty. Please do me the honor of following me to Master."

The young woman walked with tiny, graceful steps to the back door, and presented Brie to Tono. "I hope you are pleased with my work, Master."

Tono had changed into a traditional black kimono, and looked devastatingly handsome. He walked over and looked Brie over critically. His eyes on her made her even hotter for him. "Nice work, Akira. Thank you. You may leave now."

The young woman bowed and left the two alone in

Tono's backyard. Brie looked around, finally noticing the gorgeous Japanese garden. It was tiny, but the space beyond the patio was filled with exotic plants and a small waterfall. "This is lovely, Tono."

He moved up behind her and put his hands on her waist. "I am glad you like it. It does not take much to create heaven on earth."

She smiled up at him and moaned softly when he kissed her. "Oh, how I've wanted this…"

"Yes, toriko. Your spirit captured me the first day we met." He kissed her neck, sending pleasant shivers down her spine. "I plan to immortalize that spirit on film today. But first we must sit down for tea."

He gestured to a low table with two pillows. He held out his hand and helped her kneel down on one. He sat cross-legged on the other and smiled at her. "Tea is good for the soul, toriko." He poured from an earthenware pot and handed her a small cup decorated with an orchid. She smiled, recognizing the same design as on the wax she had at home.

Tono poured himself a cup as well. She waited to take a sip until he put his cup to his lips. They both swallowed the tea together, looking at each other. The brew caressed her throat like a warm blanket, and she sighed in contentment.

"Drink more, toriko," he insisted at intervals, and filled her cup several times. She didn't mind. The tea had a soothing quality to it, much like the sound of the waterfall, and she felt completely at ease.

"Do you know much about Kinbaku?" he asked.

She smiled at him bashfully. "Only what Mr. Gallant

shared in class. He said it was beautiful, though."

"Yes, my intention is to create harmonious art using the beauty of the model and the intricacy of the rope. But it is more than art, toriko. I plan to carry you to that other plane of consciousness where you can soar free."

She looked at him questioningly. "What do you mean?"

Tono took another sip of his tea and encouraged her to do the same. "This week you had Doms show you the American way to bring a submissive into subspace. Today I will show you a different way."

"How is it different?"

He reached across the small table and lightly ran his index finger down her arm before answering. "The American way is to cause pain to quickly bring a rush of endorphins into your bloodstream. My way is much more subtle, but equally effective." Brie's skin warmed at his touch, and she looked at him lustfully as he continued.

"By constraining you with rope, I will free you to enter that realm without the need of a whip or cane."

Her eyes widened. "Really?"

"Yes, toriko. The physical journey I will take you on is without violence. I hope to open up a whole new world to you." He stood up and gave her his hand. "Shall we?"

She followed him back inside his home and was surprised to see that the main room had been transformed into a photographer's studio, complete with background, lights and reflectors. In the middle of the room was a black velvet sofa, and a green straw mat covered the floor.

She looked around but did not see Akira. "Where's your assistant?"

"Normally she stays to help, but today I prefer to work alone." He placed a single finger under her chin and lifted her face up to receive his kiss. His tongue explored her mouth, tasting of green tea and manliness.

He went over to his stereo system and turned on soothing flute music. "This is a long process, toriko. It is essential that you and I are in sync." He motioned for her to kneel. He knelt behind and wrapped his arms around her, pressing Brie against his chest. "Find my breath and copy it. Breathe with me, toriko."

She was startled by his request, but calmed herself enough to listen to his breathing. She began matching her own with his. Tono's breaths were consistent and measured. She had to slow way down to harmonize. Soon she felt her entire body relax as she became one with him.

"Good…" he murmured softly. "If you feel anxious at any point, I want you to match your breath with mine."

Brie nodded. He picked up a long jute rope and showed it to her. "Today, this simple material will transport you to nirvana." She touched it and was surprised that it felt both soft and rough. "Smell it, toriko." She took in its earthy smell and smiled.

"We are all in harmony. You, me…the rope." He released her from his embrace and asked her to lift her hands in the air. He opened the kimono slightly, exposing her cleavage. Then, with an artist's precision, he began to slowly wrap her chest in a bra-like fashion. The rope crisscrossed above and below her breasts, making them stand out alluringly. Brie noticed that the rope's tight hold restricted her breathing, and it frightened her.

"Breathe with me, toriko," he reminded her. She calmed her quick, shallow breaths to match his breathing again. Instantly, she felt calmer. "What is your color?"

"Green, Tono."

He asked her to place her left hand behind her back. He took his time as he secured it to the intricate ties he'd already created. Then he held out his hand and helped her up. He guided her to the black sofa and told her to lie down on it. Tono grabbed his camera and turned on the photo lamps.

"Put your hand to your face and look at me. Imagine our first time together when you watched me take you in the mirror."

Brie's body flushed as she recalled the way he'd unleashed his passion on her, and the alluring way her tits had bounced in response to his pounding. She looked up at Tono with that image clearly planted in her mind. She ignored the camera.

"That's it…" He took several shots and then had her change poses. After a few minutes, he asked her to slide down onto the mat, and then he joined her. "Give me your other wrist."

She put it behind her back and he began an intricate lacing between both arms. It took a long time, but the feel of the rope as he tugged and pulled was relaxing. When he had finished, Tono took several pictures of her kneeling on the green mat. Then he showed her the pictures on the camera's digital screen.

Brie was amazed. The knots trailed down her back in a beautiful pattern. Just as he had made her art with wax, she was now art with rope. "It's beautiful," she murmured.

"No, little one, *you're* beautiful. The rope simply accentuates it. Close your eyes and feel the rope. Feel the restriction and embrace it."

She did as he said. Not only was her breath restricted, but she couldn't move her arms at all. It was both alarming and thrilling. Tono took another set of pictures of her kneeling on the ground and then commented, "You're beginning to feel the call of the rope, my little slave. I can see it in your eyes. Don't fight it—give in to it."

Brie wanted to, but the tea was beginning to have an undesired effect. She squirmed a little, reluctant to tell Tono that he would have to undo his elaborate binding.

He lifted her back on the couch and took several more photos, but eventually stopped. "You are not relaxed. What's blocking you?"

She was embarrassed to say it, but she could no longer remain still. She *really* needed to pee. "I'm sorry, Tono. I need to go to the bathroom. I'm so sorry, Master…"

He shook his head in amusement. "No need to be sorry, toriko." He picked her up off the couch and carried her to the bathroom, plopping her down on the toilet and hiking up her kimono.

Brie's bladder was about to burst. She looked up at him in desperation.

"Pee, little one."

"I can't."

"You can and you will. You bladder isn't going to last much longer."

She felt a little escape between her legs without her consent. The tinkle echoed in the tiny bathroom and she blushed.

"That's it, toriko. Your Master wants you to pee so he can get back to his work."

She threw caution to the wind and relaxed, letting a solid and overly long stream flow into the toilet.

Tono smiled approvingly. "Now, that wasn't so bad, was it?"

He set me up! That was the reason he'd kept refilling her cup.

Tono lifted her off the toilet when she was done, and cleaned her off thoroughly with the gentle touch of a lover. Instead of feeling embarrassed, she felt cared for and cherished.

"Thank you, Tono."

"My pleasure, toriko."

"No, I mean thank you for helping me face that obstacle. I didn't realize you knew."

"The Doms who bid for you know the progress of your training, my slave. That is why so many want you." He looked at her lustfully. "Are you ready for more?"

She nodded and followed him out of the bathroom. He led her to the couch and asked her to bend over the overstuffed arm. She heard the swish of silk and then felt his hard cock press against her moist entrance. "You will find that being taken while bound like this feels completely different."

Brie moaned as he slowly pushed into her. He was right; it was strangely exhilarating to be penetrated while tightly restricted. She couldn't adjust or scream because the rope's tight constriction didn't allow for it. She could only lie there and enjoy his manly onslaught.

Brie felt delightfully helpless. Tears ran down her face from the sheer joy of her powerlessness. "I love it, Tono," she breathed softly.

"I know, toriko. You and I are in harmony." His cock stroked her leisurely at first and then he slowly built up to a burst of energy, letting out a flood of lust that left her breathless. She rode the wave of his lovemaking, thoroughly mesmerized. He groaned as he came, his hot seed bursting deep inside her. Then he stopped, his cock still hard. Just like the time before, her body began to tense around him and pleasant chills took over.

"Yes, my slave…"

She whimpered when her clit began to pulsate and then her inner muscles started their rhythmic dance around his cock as she climaxed. He kissed the nape of her neck, growling softly until her orgasm spent itself.

He caressed her ass as he pulled out, and then cleaned her again. Tono picked up the camera. "Look into the lens, little one. I want to capture that fresh-come look."

She smiled at the camera with no need to pose. She was satiated and it radiated from her naturally.

"So beautiful, toriko," he said repeatedly as he continued to shoot.

He put the camera down and grabbed another piece

of rope. "Now, I will heighten your arousal."

He told her to lean back. The way in which he had tied her arms allowed them to support her now. He took hold of her ankle and bent her leg so that her ankle rested against the inner thigh of the same leg. He bound them together and then spread her leg out, securing it to the other rope with another set of decorative knots. When he stepped away to get his camera, Brie couldn't help herself. She tried to struggle against the constriction, but the jute held her tightly in its grip. A gush of wetness ran down the crease of her ass. She loved being at the mercy of the rope. Brie threw her head back and moaned in satisfaction.

"Don't move. That's lovely." She lay perfectly still as he preserved her state of bliss on film. She thought he was going to start on the other leg and squealed when she felt him lick her sex.

"Oh, too much, too much!" Brie's clit was extra sensitive in the wake of his pounding. She didn't think her poor body could handle being eaten.

His chuckle was low and vibrated on her clit. "That is the beauty of the rope, little one. I am in control. I say when it is enough." His tongue swirled around her clit and outer folds, tasting her juices. When he began sucking, it sent a shockwave through her. She tried to pull away, but all he had to do was hold down her untied leg and he was free to continue. She whimpered and begged him to stop as the feeling grew stronger. It didn't feel like a normal orgasm approaching, and it unnerved her.

"Please, Tono. Stop," she whimpered.

He ignored her pleas. Whatever it was, it was coming over her and she was powerless to prevent it. When it hit, time stopped for Brie. An ice-cold wave gripped her body and held her in its grasp. Her pussy contracted in response and refused to stop.

She made little mewing sounds, unable to speak—to think. She was at the mercy of this new orgasm, and Tono's constant suction was the source. He kept her there for an undeterminable amount of time and then broke away. Slowly, she felt herself returning to earth.

He helped her sit up and wound the rope over her eyes to make a blindfold. He lay her back down, and she vaguely heard Tono moving around as he took more photos. Then his gentle hands took hold of her unbound ankle and began the process of restraining it. Her body trembled under his touch, familiar with the remarkable power he had over her.

Tono murmured praises as he took additional photos, but she was floating and could hardly make out what he was saying. She didn't respond to him until she felt his lips on her clit again. "Ohhh…"

He took her on a journey back to that place where pleasure meets otherworldliness. His tongue kept her there for so long that she barely noticed when he broke away. But she smiled when she felt his manhood slide into her heaven to join her. Together, they rode the tide of pleasure as one. He was a part of her. They were conjoined in a way she had never experienced. If she had been able to, she would have wrapped her arms around him and drawn him even farther into herself.

Brie became lost in the sensations and was surprised

when she opened her eyes to find herself in Tono's bed, wrapped in his arms instead of the rope.

"You're back."

She looked into his brown eyes and sighed contentedly. "Whatever that was, whatever you did… It was amazing."

"I'm glad you respond so well to the call of the jute, toriko. Most do not embrace it as fully as you."

"How did I get here?" she asked, looking around his bedroom.

"I cut you from the ropes when I saw how deep you were into subspace. We've been lying together for over a half-hour."

"I'm sorry."

"No need to be, little one. Watching you fly is beautiful. I thoroughly enjoyed myself."

A giant yawn escaped her lips. She covered her mouth and apologized again.

He put a finger to them. "No more apologies. I'm not surprised you are tired. You've had quite a journey." His finger left a trail of tingling sensation on her lips. "I will call for a cab."

She was disappointed he wanted her to leave so soon, and he must have read it on her face.

He smiled with open affection. "I want to drive you home, toriko, but it would not be deemed appropriate." He tugged on the collar around her neck. "I cannot fraternize with you beyond the confines of the school until your training is complete." He glanced over at the clock on his nightstand. "According to the clock, it's getting close to twelve. Class ends at midnight, does it not?"

She nodded her head glumly.

"So, I will call the cab and while we wait for it to arrive, we can discuss the scene together. I promised your trainers we would, and I do not break my promises." He looked deep into her eyes, "My word is my honor."

"I know, Tono. That tongue of yours is honorable in so many ways."

He threw back his head and laughed. It pleased her to hear his laughter. She wanted to hear more, but he got up to telephone the cab. As he walked away, she noticed he was naked. She admired his tight, round ass. *So fine.* An ass she wouldn't mind waking up to every morning…

Twenty minutes later, she was back in her school uniform and heading to her apartment. She quickly texted Lea, figuring that she and Mary would just be leaving the Center.

Hey girl! You two wanna come to my place? We can film how our days went.

Her phone soon buzzed back.

Mary said she'll come, but she isn't going to record herself.

Tell her that she's a pussy.

I told her, but also added that pussies are welcome at your place.

LOL… That they are! See you soon.

Brie rested her head against the car window for the rest of the drive, lost in thought. Up until this point, her loyalty had belonged exclusively to Sir—it hadn't even been in question. However, today Tono had managed to change that, and she was falling hard.

Staring out into the dark, Brie wondered if her heart could survive being devoted to two Masters, knowing one day that she would have to choose. A tear traveled down her cheek. She whispered into the night, the declaration spoken out of desperation. "I still love you, Sir."

Navigating the Vanilla World

Brie was wrestling with her new feelings for Tono. The day she'd met Sir, she had known he was *the One*. Tono had simply been the gorgeous Dom she'd wanted to play with. However, after spending Auction Day with him, she couldn't get Tono out of her mind…or her heart. He had introduced her to the seductive art of Kinbaku, or Japanese bondage. The call of the rope, combined with his skill, had opened her eyes to another world—one that now haunted her thoughts constantly.

Sir was a powerful magnet. Her soul longed to be dominated by him in every way. Tono's call was different—more like the ocean. He beckoned her to lose herself in the waves of their harmony.

Her conflicting emotions caused her to be distracted at work. Mr. Reynolds jokingly commented as he handed the inventory sheet back to her, "Another exciting weekend, Brie?" She was in charge of ordering stock and, looking over the sheet, she saw that she'd forgotten to include several brands they were running low on.

Brie sighed. "I'm sorry." Mr. Reynolds was a kind boss and rewarded her hard work with regular raises. She hated letting him down. "I'll double-check the orders before I send them out."

"See that you do," Mr. Reynolds said, then as an afterthought he added, "You mentioned that you were taking training classes at night. Are you enrolled in extra film courses or something?"

Brie was unprepared for his question and just stood there, smiling like an idiot, while she formulated an answer. She played with the collar around her neck as she spoke. "Actually, the classes are going to help with my film career, Mr. Reynolds. Thank you for asking."

She figured she wasn't *really* lying. The documentary she was filming, based on her experiences at the Submissive Training Center, would help her career. She was confident she could snag the interest of someone in the industry when she was done. It was Brie's destiny to open the eyes of America to the hidden lifestyle.

"So when is your boyfriend coming to the shop? I still haven't given my approval yet," Mr. Reynolds said teasingly.

His protective nature was endearing. However, there was no way the old man would approve of her new BDSM lifestyle, nor would he understand there wasn't just one Dom she was attracted to at the moment. Nobody in the 'vanilla world' could relate to what she was going through. It was a lonely feeling.

Brie growled under her breath when she saw Blue Eyes at the door of the Training Center later that evening. He might think he was all cute with his daily flirting, but she had no patience for him now. Her heart was torn between two worthy men. That boy had absolutely no chance with her, and she needed to put a stop to it.

Brie took on a Mary-like stance, putting her hands on her waist and cocking her hip to one side. "Whatever you are trying to do here, Todd, it needs to stop! I have no interest in you." She powered past him and headed towards the elevator.

"Has anyone ever told you how sexy you look when you're pissed?" he called after her.

She had to bite her tongue to stop her foul-mouthed reply. Brie just threw her hand up in the air in a dismissive manner. Her training as a submissive definitely helped her maintain control as she escaped to the elevator.

She sat down in Mr. Gallant's classroom, transfixed by the pile of papers on his desk—their evaluations from the last auction. What had Tono said? He was a Kinbakushi, after all; trained to bring his models to that spiritual level of harmony. Maybe it wasn't unusual for him.

She held her breath as Mr. Gallant handed over her evaluation. "An eight, Miss Bennett? Highly unusual for your third auction. Take it as a compliment from an admirer, but do not let it go to your head. You have much to learn yet."

She looked up at him. "I agree, Mr. Gallant."

He nodded and moved on to pass out the remaining two packets. Brie dove into her evaluation, her heart pumping as she did. 'Miss Bennett has a rare gift with the rope. Able to connect on a level seldom experienced by this Master.' 'Both independent and trusting.'

She finally got to his criticisms. 'Hesitated to state need for urination. Spoiled several shots because of strained look.' Brie giggled under her breath. 'Lack of experience holds her back, but is charming to overcome as a Dom.' Tono had added at the end of the evaluation, 'Hope to work with toriko again. Could easily make a career of Kinbaku.'

Brie imagined herself joining Tono on the stage at one of his live performances and felt her heart quicken at the thought of a future with the man.

Mr. Gallant's lesson centered on living the Dom/sub lifestyle daily in the vanilla world. "When maintaining the relationship in a world of bills, friends and family, your goal should be to intertwine the lifestyle into your everyday life. Many D/s couples choose to live with two separate worlds, but it does not have to be that way. You can weave it into your day so that even in the most common situation, the D/s element is still apparent. Find a comfortable fit and be willing to change and grow as issues arise."

Mary raised her hand, waiting to be called on. "What if you don't want your family or friends discovering your secret?"

"The power play can be subtle, Miss Wilson. Something no one would think twice about. For example, you go out to eat and wait for your Dom's permission to take the first bite. You play with your napkin and talk to the guests at the table until you see his nod." Mr. Gallant leaned against his desk. "No one is the wiser but the couple maintains the bond. It's a matter of simple adjustments, but requires communication and creativity on both sides to make it work."

A shiver traveled down Brie's spine at the thought of being a submissive twenty-four seven. What would it be like to be under a Dom's rule in front of unsuspecting people?

"Tonight you will be meeting with an assigned trainer and discussing his or her expectations of your behavior in public. You will then go downtown and interact as you have been instructed." He smiled at the girls. "It should be a real eye-opening experience."

The three were told to meet in a new classroom on the other side of the school. Brie and her classmates chattered nervously as they made their way through the hallways. Pleasing their Doms in the outside world would be a challenging assignment indeed!

Brie was surprised to see there was a fifth trainer at the table as they walked into the classroom. She stood in respectful silence, sneaking peeks at the dark-haired Dom. He had a classic, model-type face and spoke in a deep voice that demanded attention.

Sir addressed the group of students. "I would like to introduce Master Anderson. He will be running a Training Center of his own and has joined us for the next few weeks to observe and help train this class. Although he is new to this Center, he is an experienced Dom and I expect you to give him the same respect you give all trainers here. Do you understand?"

All three girls answered in unison, "Yes, Sir."

Master Anderson stood up. He towered above the

others, which highlighted just how tall the guy was. "I do not take this responsibility lightly. I shall train you well, but in turn I expect complete obedience."

Brie suddenly felt the urge to bow to her new trainer. She followed that gut instinct and knelt before him. The other girls followed suit.

She felt him approach and then he asked in a deep baritone, "What is your name?"

"Brie Bennett, Master Anderson."

"Look at me, young Brie."

She looked up into his intense green eyes. *Damn, he is good-looking.* Not as handsome as Sir, of course, but…close.

"I appreciate a slave who understands the importance of a bow." He nodded once before turning from her and sitting back down.

Such a simple interaction, but it had made her all shaky inside. She noticed that Sir patted Master Anderson on the back, as if they were old friends. It was such an endearing gesture that she almost burst out in a smile.

Sir looked pleased when he caught Brie's eye. "Class, I will be staying behind to walk Master Anderson through our school. Miss Wilson, you will partner with Master Coen for this practicum. Ms. Taylor, you'll be with Ms. Clark, and Miss Bennett will work with Marquis Gray." He paused as he looked each of the girls over. "Take this opportunity to discuss protocols and ask questions before you head out. Pay particular attention to your trainer's instructions. You will be critiqued on how well you blend into the vanilla world while fulfilling your Dom's protocols."

Brie was disappointed to see Sir stand up with the new trainer and leave. Her eyes followed Sir until they rested on Marquis Gray, who happened to be staring at her intently. "Pearl, are you ready to learn my demands?"

She blushed at being caught ogling Sir. Nothing escaped Marquis' sharp eyes. "Yes, Master."

After a half-hour of discussion and a visit to the bathroom to follow an order from him, Marquis handed her more casual attire. It consisted of a simple black cocktail dress and four-inch heels. *Such a luxury!* She quickly dressed under his watchful eye, and then he escorted her out of the Center with the two other girls and their trainers.

Brie's heart hammered in her chest as she held onto the arm of Marquis, whom she was to call 'Mister' Gray for the evening. He had commanded that she maintain contact with him in some form at all times. She was excited about the challenge and appreciated the fact he wanted her to touch him in public.

Instead of taking a car like the other two trainers, he took her to the bus stop in front of the school to wait. Brie watched Lea follow Ms. Clark to her car. Apparently, the Domme preferred her sub to walk behind her. Mary walked beside Master Coen without touching him. Looking at the four of them, Brie did not see anything unusual. No one would suspect the D/s dynamics going on.

When the bus pulled up, Marquis Gray boarded first. Brie grabbed onto the belt loop of his dark pants and sat beside him with her thigh pressed against his. He did not look at her, did not respond to her in the slightest, but she was a bundle of excitement knowing they were touching. The contact was such an intimate yet subtle exchange.

She met the gaze of a man sitting opposite her. She quickly glanced away, but gasped loudly when she felt the vibration of the toy strapped against her clit. She clutched Marquis Gray's thigh as he ramped up the speed of the little device. He leaned over and whispered, "No coming."

Brie nodded as she dug her fingernails into his leg and struggled not to whimper. The buzzing was so loud that she was certain everyone on the bus could hear it, but other than the man sitting across from them, no one paid any attention.

Marquis changed the rhythm to pulsing and she groaned softly. Being in public and having someone watch but be unaware of their unique exchange was thrilling. The bus slowed down, as did the vibrator, until it eventually stopped. Marquis stood up and Brie placed her hand lightly on his back as they made their way off the bus.

He held out his arm gallantly and she wrapped herself around it. She looked at all the people walking in the opposite direction. Everyone seemed in a rush to get somewhere, while the two of them strolled at a relaxed pace amongst the multitudes. She caught the eye of an agitated businessman and smiled in sympathy.

Brie stumbled when the vibration hit.

"No fair, Mister Gray," she whimpered, straightening herself back up and trying to walk with grace while her pussy tingled in delight.

"Completely fair, pearl."

They walked down the crowded sidewalk, heading towards the music and lights of the downtown scene. He hadn't told her what his plans were, which only added another layer of excitement to this practicum.

Before he guided her into an extremely popular celebrity restaurant, Marquis turned the toy down to its lowest setting. She was surprised that they were immediately seated in the corner of the crowded dining room. The table was elegantly set with a long, white tablecloth, fresh flowers and romantic candlelight.

She figured Marquis must know somebody, because it was impossible to get into the place. The fact was that Brie had never been here before, and had only heard about it from friends whose friends had managed to get in years ago.

Brie looked around, suddenly realizing she was in the presence of some very influential people. People who could make her film career a reality. The host tucked the chair behind Brie and then did the same for Marquis Gray. Remembering his command, she slipped off her shoe and ran her foot against his leg.

Her nervousness increased twofold at the knowledge that there were so many prominent people about, but Marquis' smile was easy. "See anyone you recognize, pearl?"

"Yes!" She couldn't hide her excitement at knowing directors and producers were just a few feet away. She pointed demurely at a charismatic gentleman entertaining two attractive models and whispered, "That's Mr. Holloway. He's the producer of not just one, but two of the most popular cable series running right now."

"Is he? Well, then, I would suggest being discreet when you crawl under the table and take me into your mouth."

Brie stared at him in shock. *Here in the crowded restaurant?* What kind of impression would that make on the very people she needed to impress? She hesitated and his eyes bored into her. "Which is it, pearl? Are you my submissive or not?"

She closed her eyes. This was so much bigger than a simple sexual request, and she felt chills of indecision consume her. It was a defining moment for Brie, and she knew it—one of those forks in the road where, once the decision was made, there would be no turning back.

Brie finally opened her eyes and looked around the dining room. People were engrossed in conversations or staring at menus. Being in the corner, she and Marquis Gray were not that noticeable. Of course, there were the random people walking to and fro, but she would just have to take a chance with them. With a casualness she did not feel, she dropped her napkin and bent down to pick it up. In the process, she lifted the linen tablecloth as if it were an ordinary thing to do, and ducked under the table.

Once she found herself hidden from view under the table, Brie felt the thrill of her assignment. She crawled between Marquis' legs and slowly unzipped his slacks. The simple action was made difficult due to the bulge in his pants, but feeling the rigidity of his shaft made her even wetter. This scenario was equally exciting for them both.

She freed his cock from his briefs and was just about to place the head of his shaft into her mouth when she heard the waiter return. "Are you ready to order, sir, or would you like me to wait for the young lady?"

Marquis Gray guided her mouth onto his cock with his hand at the back of her head. "I will order for both of us…"

Brie swirled her tongue around the ridge of his member before taking him deeper. Even in the shadows under the table, she could see his uniquely curved shaft. It excited her and she sucked even harder.

She was rewarded with the sound of his grunt. He adjusted the vibrator to a much faster rate and she moaned softly around his dick. When he had finished with the order and the waiter was presumably out of earshot, she heard his reminder from above: "No coming, pearl."

She opened her throat to him and took his entire shaft then. The curve of his manhood forced her to take him at a different angle, but she was still able to press her red lips against his dark pubic hair. He stiffened as she made her subtle thrusting movements while taking his cock deep in her throat. The waiter returned and asked if he would like pepper on their salads.

Brie wasn't sure how Marquis managed it, but he answered in a normal tone, "No pepper for either of us, thank you." When the man moved away, Marquis fisted her long hair and guided her. She gave in to his rhythm and pace as he leisurely face-fucked her under the table.

Brie couldn't believe that she was in the middle of a famous restaurant, deep-throating her trainer while a vibrator buzzed between her legs. It was surreal and erotic. She was almost disappointed when he came. His essence slid down her throat and she licked up any remaining traces before zipping up his pants and wiping her mouth with the napkin she'd dropped. She remained between his legs while he eased the vibrator back down to the lowest setting. Brie waited until she heard the command, "You can join me now."

Brie lifted the white cloth and as nonchalantly as she could, sat back down on the chair, placing her hand on his upper thigh. She snuck a glance in Mr. Holloway's direction and was grateful to see he was still engaged with his girls.

Marquis turned off the vibrator and looked at her knowingly. "That was not an easy command for you to follow. Do you regret it?"

Her eyes did not waver when she answered, "No, Mister Gray. I enjoyed it."

He nodded and ordered, "Eat your salad."

After dinner, they made their way back to the bus stop. The streets were still packed with people enjoying the LA nightlife. Brie noticed a sweet couple walking hand in hand. As they passed by, the girl smiled at her and the guy winked.

Marquis abruptly stopped in the middle of the sidewalk and grasped the back of her neck, kissing her deeply as he turned the vibrator on full blast. Her knees gave out, but he held her in his arms and thrust his tongue deep into her mouth. Not coming at that moment was extremely difficult—pure torture, to be exact.

He pulled away. "Nicely done, pearl. You denied

your pleasure, but I am concerned." Marquis looked into her eyes, penetrating her soul with his gaze. She could barely breathe under his intense scrutiny. "It's painfully obvious there is much for you to learn."

She wobbled in her shoes when he took away his support. He turned the vibrator to the lowest setting and held out his arm again. She took it warily and leaned against him as they walked.

She couldn't bear the thought that he still found her lacking. "What do I need to learn?" When he remained silent, she begged, "Please, Mister Gray…"

He looked down at her with stern tenderness. "The fact you would ask shows how far you have yet to go."

Brie wilted on his arm in defeat. She heard his warm chuckle. "You are unique, pearl. To many you seem wise beyond your years, but the truth is that they mistake your instincts for actual knowledge."

She expected the bus ride home to be uneventful, but she should have known better with Marquis. It was much less packed, but the group sitting opposite them must have been bored and stared at the two shamelessly.

He used the situation to challenge her. Marquis whispered in her ear, "Do you think you can come without anyone being the wiser?"

She automatically answered, "I'll try…" She was desperate to please him, but she stopped midsentence. Try was *not* an option with Marquis. She looked at him apologetically and corrected herself. "Yes, Mister Gray."

He adjusted the control in his pocket and the buzzing began. Brie turned her head to look out of the window, trying to keep a stoic face. She squeaked when he turned the vibrator up. She let her hand, which had been resting on his shoulder, travel down so she could intertwine her fingers with his. She squeezed his hand hard when he turned the vibrator up to the highest setting.

Her breaths came in desperate, muffled gasps. She pressed her thighs together and softly mewed when Marquis Gray placed his warm lips on her neck. The contact sent her over the edge and her entire body stiffened before there was a burst of release. He kissed her on the lips, making her body pulse with electricity. Brie moaned into Marquis' mouth as her body finally gave in to the luscious feeling.

When her muscles relaxed, he reached into his pocket and turned off the vibrator before sitting back in the seat. As far as the group watching was concerned, they'd just witnessed a kiss, not a sexual power play between a Dom and his submissive. Brie adored it!

She grabbed onto his belt loop when they left the bus, still riding the high from their encounter. She gratefully took the arm he offered and cuddled against him as they walked towards the Center. Brie hadn't understood just how fun living the lifestyle under the watchful eyes of the world could be. She smiled up at Marquis Gray, hoping her eyes adequately expressed her gratitude. "Thank you for tonight, *Mister.*" He gave her a wry smile at the vanilla title.

Marquis stopped just before they reached the entrance of the school and lifted her chin to look her in the eye. "There will always be more to learn, pearl. Don't ever stop, and don't you dare settle for the status quo."

He didn't let go of her chin until she'd nodded. Brie couldn't help wondering if he was talking about her growth as a sub, or her future choice of Dom.

He guided her into the Center and the two made their way to the small classroom in silence. The other two girls were already standing before the panel. Brie let go of Marquis' arm and stood with her fellow students, her head bowed respectfully.

"As with every practicum, we need to discuss your performance so that you can learn from the experience," Sir reminded them. "Master Coen, why don't you start us off?"

"Fine." He laced his fingers together and stared at Mary intently as he spoke. "Miss Wilson began our outing well, remembering my protocols up until dinner. She found it amusing to try to feed me bites from her plate even after I clearly expressed my displeasure. It quickly became apparent she was seeking punishment." Master Coen's voice turned cold. "I do not care for disobedient subs, Miss Wilson—very few Doms do. Do not think for one second that you will get the punishment you were craving. There will be no spanking tonight. Instead, I will see you spend a half-hour in the stockade…alone."

Sir added, "We are training submissives, Miss Wilson. The bratty sub may be endearing to a novice, but to a true Dom such behavior is viewed as disrespectful."

"I am sorry, Master Coen," Mary said. Brie glanced sideways, surprised to see that she did not look fazed in the least. Brie figured that her indifference was a façade and that she must be mightily unhappy that she would be heading to the stockade after class.

"Marquis, can you share what you observed with Miss Bennett?"

"Unfortunately, Miss Bennett never picked up on why I was using the vibrator tonight."

Brie's heart fell. Now she, along with everyone else, would hear of her failure.

"Please elaborate," Sir stated.

The heat rose to her cheeks while she waited. It felt just like those first nights when the panel had picked her apart.

"Miss Bennett still struggles with eye contact. Even though she was in the presence of her Dom, she continued to make eye contact with other males."

Brie wanted to melt into the ground and disappear.

Ms. Clark jumped right on it, naturally. "You better explain yourself, Miss Bennett."

Brie refused to look at her, feeling completely embarrassed and ashamed. "I wasn't thinking, Ms. Clark. I just naturally look people in the eye when I am outside the Center." She sighed deeply before continuing, "Obviously, it is a habit I need to break."

"No, Miss Bennett," Sir answered. "It is not a habit you need to break. It is one you need to be aware of when you are in the presence of your Dom."

Brie was grateful that he understood it was a part of who she was. Yes, she could learn *not* to look people in the eye, just as she had inside the walls of the Training Center, but to change that natural inclination would change a fundamental part of herself.

"Is there anything else to note?" Sir asked.

"Yes, as a matter of fact there is," Marquis Gray replied amiably. "When presented with the choice of impressing potential film execs or following my order, she chose to follow my order. Although she hesitated, I was pleasantly surprised."

"Hesitated?" Ms. Clark snapped. "After how many weeks of training?"

"Although I would normally agree with you, Samantha," Marquis Gray answered, before turning his attention back to Brie, "I set the situation up specifically to see which was more important to you, Miss Bennett—your role as a sub or your potential career. I don't think even you could answer that until tonight."

Brie suddenly felt nauseated. She wasn't *only* a submissive; she still wanted a career in film.

Sir saw the devastation written on her face and a smile played across his lips. "Miss Bennett, it is not a case of either or. You can still be successful as a businesswoman as long as the Dom you select knows and agrees to support you in your career."

Master Anderson's baritone assurance followed. "You would be surprised how many prominent couples are living out the D/s lifestyle, Miss Bennett."

"Thank you," Brie said quietly, looking to the ground to hide her utter relief.

Lea was the last to be critiqued. Sir turned to their female trainer and asked, "Ms. Clark, how did Ms. Taylor do outside these walls?"

Ms. Clark seemed to glow when she spoke of Lea. "I must say, Ms. Taylor has the unique ability to read my wishes before I speak them. Had I not been with her these past few weeks, I would have mistaken her for a more experienced sub."

Brie couldn't help wondering if Lea had gotten to spend some alone time with Ms. Clark and enjoy that pretty blonde pussy. A good orgasm seemed to do wonders for Ms. Clark's attitude towards a girl, but then, she always had liked Lea.

"So, Ms. Taylor handled herself well in public?" Sir asked.

"She was practically flawless. A real treat to escort."

After Lea's positive critique, she and Brie were allowed to leave. Mary, however, was forced to follow Master Coen. She had an almost haughty air about her as she walked down the hall.

Poor Mary—she was still her own worst enemy.

Her First DP

B rie was stunned to see Blue Eyes talking to Master Anderson at the front door of the Center the next evening. The two were in an intense conversation, which she was surprised to hear was about world politics. She hadn't thought they'd notice as she passed by, but before she was through the door that Blue Eyes was holding open, he called out, "Good evening, Miss Bennett."

She was startled to feel a small thrill that he hadn't forgotten her, but did not turn around to acknowledge him. As she walked away, however, she began to feel agitated. What right did that boy have to talk to one of *her* trainers? It felt like an invasion of her space, her life. She turned around and glared at the boy. Tomorrow she was going to give him a piece of her mind—right between the eyes.

After Mr. Gallant's class, the girls headed to the auditorium. Brie enjoyed practicums there, because they tended to be the most elaborate and exciting.

The girls sat down and Lea was the first called onto the stage. "We noticed last week that you had a particular affinity towards the violet wand," Sir explained.

Brie saw her friend quiver in anticipation. "Yes, Sir."

"We felt it only fair that you enjoy the instrument under the hands of a master."

An older gentleman entered the stage. He had an Obi-Wan Kenobi vibe to him because of the large, hooded robe he wore.

"Undress and lie down, pet," he commanded Lea. She artfully removed her clothes and then lay down on a bench. It was so low that her feet touched the floor. He tied her ankles to the legs of the bench, as well as her wrists, so that all of Lea's womanly parts were open and exposed. Brie could see her large, unnatural breasts rising and falling rapidly. It was obvious to Brie, even from her seat, how excited Lea was.

There was a case on a small table, which her Dom opened. He attached a round glass ball and plugged in the device. Instantly, a buzzing sound filled the auditorium. "We'll start you off slow, pet," he said in a low, ominous tone.

Brie shifted in her seat, getting turned on by Lea's scene. Her friend made a light whimper when the wand touched her stomach. He ran the wand over her skin, from her thighs to her fingertips. "Color?"

"Green, Master."

"Call me Dominus," he said as he turned up the intensity, letting a spark fly from the wand to her left nipple.

She squealed before she answered. "Yes, Dominus."

"You enjoy the electricity—in fact, I would say you crave it," he murmured, keeping the wand from her.

Her body writhed on the bench. "I do, Dominus. I *crave* the wand."

He allowed another spark to fly, caressing her right nipple with the tiny stream of purple light. Lea's moan of ecstasy reached Brie's groin.

The wand made a slow and sensual descent to her nether regions, crackling as it went. Both Mary and Brie were on the edge of their seats by the time they heard Lea's squeal of pleasure.

Dominus turned the wand off, leaving Lea gasping in desperation. He then attached another device and slipped it into his pocket. He looked at both Brie and Mary and informed them, "I have just electrified myself." He attached metal talons to his fingers and smiled wickedly. "Everything I touch becomes a conduit and will feel the bite." He turned back to Lea.

She struggled as he approached her, but moaned loudly when he raked his fingers over her skin with the electrified claws. He played with her nipples, making her buck and squirm. "Yes, Dominus," she cried.

Brie found herself equally caught up in the scene. She cringed when the Dom traced one finger down Lea's neck, lingering around the swell of her breasts and then tickling her bellybutton. He dragged his fingers up the insides of her thighs, teasing as he got ever closer to her sex. She was begging for more when he stopped and removed the talons. Next, he picked up a small metal whip with two tails made of metal chains. He glided them over her skin, causing her to whimper and gasp.

Just when Brie thought Lea couldn't take any more, Dominus untied her and commanded that she present herself. She moved unsteadily as she got down on all fours and offered herself to him. He opened his robe and engulfed them both, hiding their movements under the cloak. It was incredibly erotic to hear her passionate moans but not see what was happening underneath.

Brie bit her lip, aching with need. Their cries of a shared orgasm soon filled the tiny theater. Brie sat back, frustrated and unsatisfied. She would have to give electricity a try. Until tonight, it hadn't interested her in the least.

After their scene, the stage was cleared and reset with a bed and side table. Brie crossed her fingers. The sexual tension straining in her body screamed to be unleashed.

"Miss Bennett, make your way to the stage," Sir instructed.

Brie had to compose herself, straightening her skirt and walking slowly up the steps. From the other side she saw Baron climbing the stairs. Brie quickly glanced down at the floor, excited at the prospect of another session with him.

When he reached her side, he ran his fingers over her arm. She loved the sharp contrast of his chocolate skin against her creamy white. "Baron," she purred, lifting her eyes to look into his beautiful hazel ones.

"We meet again," he said with a grin.

She echoed his smile, grateful to be partnered with her dark Dom. However, Brie was so hot and bothered she was worried that she would not be able to hold back her orgasm if he demanded it of her. Especially when his thick lips landed on her mouth and that wicked tongue tasted her. She trembled in his arms, a hotbed of lustful desire.

He ordered her to undress. As she folded her clothes in a tidy heap, he removed his briefs, exposing his thick shaft. He sat down on the bed and motioned her to him. She walked over, swaying her hips sensually, wondering how he was going to use her.

"Kneel."

She immediately bowed at his feet and he tied a blindfold over her eyes. She heard him move farther onto the bed, and then he directed her, "Come to me. Lick my balls and suck my cock, kitten, before I ask you to impale yourself."

Brie purred, loving his command. She held out her hands and found the edge of the bed. She crawled onto it and made her way between his legs. She kept her ass in the air as she bent down to lick his balls. They were salty from sweat. She caressed both with her tongue, moaning as she pleased him with her mouth, needing him to hear her pleasure.

"Suck me."

She took his shaft in one hand and repositioned herself over his cock. Gliding her lips over his shaft, she fluttered her tongue over the frenulum. His intake of breath turned her on and she sucked him with more enthusiasm. Soon, however, he commanded her to stop.

"Impale yourself, kitten."

Brie's loins contracted in pleasure. She blindly climbed on top of Baron and rubbed her moist pussy over his shaft. Bracing her legs, she slowly guided the head of his generous manhood into her. Brie paused just before she descended onto his hard cock, letting it fill her completely. She ground herself onto his base and sighed in contentment.

Baron grabbed her hips and began pumping her up and down on his shaft. "I have something new planned. Something you haven't tried before."

Her interest was piqued. Whatever it was, she completely trusted Baron.

"Lay your head on my chest," he ordered huskily.

With his cock still lodged inside her, Brie laid her cheek against Baron's muscular frame. He wrapped his arms around her possessively and held her there. She could hear his heart beating loud and clear, bringing a sense of peace to her neediness.

Then she felt *his* touch…

Brie gasped when he ran his hand over the curve of her ass. The trail of tingling sensations left in the wake of his hand left her with no doubt as to whom it was. She whispered, "Sir…"

"Yes, Brie."

Her whole body became an electrical current, making it almost impossible to breathe.

"You will be taking both of us at the same time," he said smoothly, as his hand continued to leave a trail of fire on her skin.

"Yes, Sir." She licked her lips, not quite believing what was happening. She had been whipped, spanked, and even fucked by a colossal cock, but *never* by two men at once.

The idea of taking Sir with Baron still deep inside her was frighteningly erotic and it made her gush with wetness. "She's ready, Thane," she heard Baron say beneath her.

Sir confidently replied, "I know she is. I can tell she's hungry for it."

Brie heard the slippery sound of lube and imagined Sir coating his princely cock with his masculine hand. Brie whimpered softly into Baron's chest.

"Relax, kitten." Baron chuckled lightly. "You are about to please your two favorite Doms. A submissive's dream."

The bed moved as Sir positioned himself behind her. He lightly touched her tight hole, coating it with lube before he slipped a finger inside. She mewed softly as his finger covered the walls of her taut ass. It felt completely different from before. Her pussy was already stretched fully by Baron's thick shaft, making Sir's simple finger penetration more pronounced.

"Relax, Brie. I always start off slow," Sir reminded her.

His rich voice calmed her and she felt her body respond to it. She was desperate to feel Sir inside her. "I *need* to please you, Sir," she implored.

"You will," he replied confidently.

He pressed the head of his shaft against her tight sphincter. Her body resisted his invasion, even though she longed for it. He began slapping her ass lightly. "Let me in, Brie." The gentle slapping relaxed her muscles and she gasped as the tip of his cock disappeared inside.

"Good girl," Baron praised beneath her. His hands ran lightly over her skin as Sir pressed his shaft deeper into her ass.

Sir's grunts of pleasure almost undid Brie. Her body

willingly opened itself up even though it was being stretched beyond capacity. She felt him push in farther and she whimpered.

"You're so sexy, kitten," Baron murmured, lifting his head up and finding her lips. They kissed as Sir gently thrust his shaft deeper into her tight ass. She groaned into Baron's mouth, excited to be taking both cocks at once.

"Put your hands behind your back," Sir commanded.

When Brie did, he crossed her small wrists and held them against her back with one hand. The feeling of restraint excited Brie and she felt another wave of moisture coat Baron's cock.

"She likes that," Baron commented.

"I know exactly what this submissive needs." Sir grabbed a fistful of her hair with his other hand and turned her face towards him. His kiss was demanding and passionate. A flood of emotion passed between their lips. When he pulled away, she was shaking from the intensity of it.

He immediately began stroking her ass with his rigid cock as he held her wrists behind her back. After several lengthy thrusts, Baron took hold of her hips and joined Sir, the two thrusting in opposite rhythms.

Brie's whole body tingled as she took the manly thrusts of both Doms. The heated groans and grunts of the two Dominants blessed her submissive heart. She soon joined her voice with theirs as her body relaxed and took their passionate assault.

After several minutes of the pounding, Sir let go of her wrists and asked Baron to help him. She felt Baron lift her by the torso while Sir gathered her into his arms and held her against his chest. It gave the three completely new angles to enjoy and allowed Baron access to her clit. His hand reached between her legs and began stoking the fire. "There is no escape," she heard him growl.

She whimpered against Sir as Baron flicked his fingers expertly, making her pussy sing. "You come first," Sir commanded. Both men stopped thrusting.

Baron concentrated on her clit while Sir let his hands rove over her breasts, caressing, pinching and tugging. "Come for me, Brie," Sir whispered.

Brie leaned against his shoulder, letting out a cry of frustration and deep emotion. "Yes," he growled into her neck. "Let it out, Brie. Release…"

Her body contracted violently against both cocks, caressing them with her orgasm. Sir pushed her back down onto Baron and the two men began thrusting into her. Her body was now open and ready to receive their gifts. Brie verbalized her ecstasy as Baron climaxed inside her, the auditorium echoing with her impassioned cries.

Sir slowly pulled out. "I am going to come all over your sweet ass." She felt the burst of warm liquid on her skin. It felt as if he was marking her as his, and she moaned in delight. He rubbed his cock over her, spreading his seed on her skin.

Once he had moved away, Baron lifted her off his spent shaft. She took the blindfold off and dressed, purposely leaving Sir's essence on her. She stood between the two Doms and faced the panel.

Master Coen asked, "How would you rate the scene,

Miss Bennett?"

"A nine."

"What did you find particularly satisfying about it?"

"It was heady trying something new, but the opportunity to please two Doms… Over the top."

Ms. Clark responded dryly, "It is a highly unusual scenario, Miss Bennett. I wouldn't get used to it."

"Most Doms will *not* share a female like that," Marquis Gray stated with a hint of disdain.

Brie wondered if it was jealousy on his part or a rivalry between him and Sir. Brie remembered that Marquis had warned her once that he would never DP her with Sir.

Master Coen answered, "It is different in training circumstances and you know it. Get off your high-horse, Gray." Then Master Coen glared at Brie, as if to say, *This is all your fault!*

The new trainer, Master Anderson, took the reins. "Your interest in pleasing both Doms is admirable, Miss Bennett. However, I noticed one was more attended to than the other."

Brie blanched. Had she been obvious? If so, there was a chance she could be kicked out of the program now that she had riled Master Coen up again. "Master Anderson, I don't understand. Can you please explain?" she asked.

"It appeared to me that your attention was focused mainly on Baron, so that Headmaster Davis was forced to demand his needs."

Marquis Gray looked at the new trainer in disbelief, but said nothing.

"Actually, Thane took over the scene. He overflexed his dominance, but you'll get no complaints from me about kitten." Baron leaned over and kissed Brie full on the lips, leaving her smiling with relief when he pulled away.

Ms. Clark brushed the whole topic away with one simple comment. "It doesn't matter. The next time Miss Bennett enjoys double penetration, it will most likely be with two dildos."

Sir sounded amused when he replied, "Quite right."

He placed his hand momentarily on the small of Brie's back, directing her off the stage, and then he dropped his hand away. To lose Sir's touch again was devastating, and it highlighted that she was still very much his devoted sub.

Oh, Sir…

What the Hell Are
You Doing Here?

B rie was set to give Blue Eyes, a.k.a. Todd Wallace, a piece of her mind and she knew it wasn't going to be pretty. However, it was imperative she make that boy understand he needed to leave her (and anyone even remotely connected to her) alone.

But as she walked up to the doors of the Center, she noticed Blue Eyes wasn't there. She was thrown by the disappointment she felt as she opened the door for herself and walked inside the school. She shook her head, berating her stupid emotions. *Good grief, Brie, it's what you wanted. You just psyched yourself for a big blowout and didn't get it. Boo hoo.*

She sat down in class and Lea immediately asked, "What's wrong, Brie?"

"Nothing. Why?"

Mary quipped, "Oh, I don't know. You look like your cat just died or something."

Brie turned her back on them both. "Whatever."

"Gee, Brie, you're starting to sound like me," Mary sniped.

Thankfully, Mr. Gallant started the class and stopped the unwelcomed conversation. "BDSM clubs have specific rules that must be followed. Each club is different, but there are some basics you should follow. Normally, only those invited to the club by a friend can attend. Random gawkers are *not* appreciated. If you witness something shocking to you, keep it to yourself or leave. Standing around watching the scene with your jaw hanging open or telling others how uncomfortable you feel watching it is considered rude.

"You should also be aware that drugs and alcohol are not allowed. They are unnecessary and dangerous in this environment. Normally, there is no sex allowed for either the spectators or performers."

He noticed Mary's look of disbelief and asked, "Does that surprise you, Miss Wilson?"

She nodded. "It does, Mr. Gallant. I assumed everyone was having sex in those places."

"A common misconception," he replied. "Although there are a few clubs in the area that do allow the performers to engage in sexual play during a scene, it is unusual."

He continued with the rules. "If you must speak while watching a scene, do so in quiet tones or walk to a social area. You do not want to distract either the Dom or the sub. If you feel there is an issue, contact a staff member. *Never* interrupt the scene unless the Dom asks for help. It is also important to stay a proper distance away for safety reasons. You do not want to find yourself in the path of a whip." He made the motion of cracking a whip. The flick of his wrist was so quick that Brie had no doubt her teacher knew how to wield one. She wiggled in her seat, liking the idea.

"After the scene is over, be respectful and leave the couple alone until they are back in the social area. It is completely fine to compliment a Dom if you have enjoyed a particular scene. However, you are not allowed to talk to or touch any sub without asking the permission of the Dominant in charge."

Mr. Gallant looked sternly at Lea. "I hope you have been paying close attention, Ms. Taylor." Brie's breath caught when she heard her teacher's next words. "Because tomorrow we will not be meeting here. Instead, we will be meeting at a local club so that you can experience firsthand the pleasures of public display. It is not for everyone, but many in the BDSM culture find it *quite* entertaining."

Brie was a mess after his announcement. The idea of witnessing different scenes with other D/s couples in the community was almost more than she could handle. How would it be different from the Center? Would the club look like a dungeon with different cells? Would the air be full of the sounds of submissives screaming in pleasure? What would it *smell* like?

When the lesson ended, Brie skipped alongside the other two girls. "We're going to go to a real dungeon! Wait, do you think that's what they're called? Anyway…can you believe it?"

Lea looked as excited as Brie. "Man, I can just imagine being tied up and flogged by Marquis Gray in front of everyone."

"I know!" Brie exclaimed.

Mary looked disinterested. "I don't know what you're making such a big deal for. You exhibitionists or something?"

Brie slammed her hip into Mary, making her lose balance. "Don't pretend for a second you aren't interested. I can tell you love playing out a good scene in front of us. Hello! I've only been watching you the last few weeks."

Mary gave her a snide look just before they walked into the classroom. It was the same one they'd used on their first night, the one with the spongy floor and large, triangular ramps. Brie was puzzled when she saw a second table with four empty chairs on the opposite side of the room. Something weird was going on.

"Tonight you are going to have the opportunity to work with and rate training Doms. A reverse of what you have experienced up to this point."

All three girls shifted their stances. It seemed crazy! They were being given the chance to rate their Masters for a change?

Sir spoke solemnly. "You may not be aware, but we have similar training for Doms on this campus. Their sessions start after you are in class and end after you leave. Chances are you have not come in contact with these men, but you will be introduced tonight. Take the responsibility we are giving you seriously, just as the Doms have who've rated you. Each of you knows personally the impact a rating has on the recipient. Understand, we will not allow you to evaluate the Doms until after they leave the room and you are *not* allowed to top from the bottom."

Brie hated to be the idiot of the bunch, but she needed to know. "Sir?"

"Yes, Miss Bennett?"

"Can you explain what topping from the bottom means?"

"Certainly. I was waiting for one of you to ask. Topping is a term used to describe a submissive taking control of a scene while still playing the submissive. Unless the Dominant has specifically asked for your help and/or instruction, a sub should never top from the bottom. Tonight you are to do everything asked of you without hesitation, unless safety is involved. In that case, we expect you to call out the safe word."

Sir got up and walked over to the three. "Ladies, just because we are asking you to assess student Doms does not give you the right to treat them with any less respect. Know that we are watching your interaction with them as much as their interaction with you."

"Yes, Sir," the three answered in unison.

Brie couldn't believe her luck. The chance to rate a partner's performance was an unexpected gift for a submissive. The night just kept getting better and better!

Sir sat back down and gestured towards the door. Four trainers came in and sat down—three males and one female, similar to their own panel. Right behind them came three Doms. Brie averted her eyes, fighting the urge to take a quick peek. She stared at her Dom's brown loafers and black pants, waiting for his permission.

"Look at me, blossom."

Brie looked up into his crystal blue eyes and stopped breathing. *You…! What the hell are you doing here?*

Todd met her gaze and said in an authoritative voice, "I have waited patiently for this day."

Brie took a gasp of air. "I don't understand…"

"I will explain, but first you must undress, leaving only your stockings."

It seemed like a dream as she gracefully removed her corset, skirt, shoes and panties, placing them neatly on the floor. When she stood up, he looked her over and commented simply, "Enchanting."

Brie blushed for no good reason.

"Bow at my feet, blossom."

She did so immediately and then felt his hand on her head. He stood there and remained silent while the other Doms directed their subs to the ramps. She wasn't sure what he was waiting for.

"Master?"

"You will not call me Master. I am Faelan to you."

"Yes, Faelan."

"Come over here, blossom." He led her away from the ramp and over to a corner of the room. "Lie on your back."

While Brie did as he asked, she watched Faelan move over to a table and pick up several items from it. When he turned back towards her, she quickly snapped her head back and stared at the ceiling, trying to calm her breathing. She couldn't believe Blue Eyes was her Dom…

He walked into her line of sight and held up a thin silver bracelet in the shape of an X. "The prettiest bondage I could find."

Brie crinkled her brow, uncertain how it counted as bondage. She soon found out when he placed one of her wrists into it, crossed her other wrist over it and then locked them into place. Brie looked at her wrists, bound in thin silver, and smiled appreciatively. "Beautiful…"

"Lay your arms back above your head," he ordered, then took a scarlet rope and bound her ankles together. He took another tie and bound her knees.

He looked over his work with approval. Then he held up a large, fluffy white feather and twirled it between his fingers. "My instrument of pleasure for tonight."

It took everything in Brie not to burst out laughing. *A feather? Seriously?* She had been flogged and caned, and he was going to tease her with a feather? Blue Eyes had no idea how pathetically cute he was.

"Lift your head up, blossom."

She did as he asked and he placed an eye mask over her head. It smelled of lavender. He placed it firmly over her eyes, blocking all light, before gently laying her head back down on the spongy floor. The blindfold, in addition to the bindings, had an effect on her. She was suddenly very aware she was under his power.

She expected his hands on her naked body, but instead he settled down beside her. The smell of him was familiar—manly and intoxicating. "I will explain now, as I caress your skin."

Brie felt hundreds of tickling points as he moved the feather over her breast. She gasped in delight, surprised at the sensual feel of it. While the feather glided over her skin, he drew her in with his low, masculine tone. "The moment you landed in my arms at the front of the school, I became captivated by you."

He used the tip of the feather to tease her nipple. It

hardened from the attention. Then she felt the warmth of his lips on her nipple. It was just for an instant, and suddenly the feather was back, teasing her again. She sighed in frustration.

"When I realized you were training to be a submissive it was as if all the pieces of a puzzle came together for me. My need to dominate finally made sense and my path was clear. I contacted Thane Davis and expressed my desire to train at the school. It wasn't an easy sell because the class had started a few days before."

He stopped, and her attention focused on the caress of the feather against the side of her hip. The tingling trail it left was followed by another warm kiss.

"I offered to drop my advanced business classes for a semester and put in extra time to make up for starting behind. It took convincing, but I finally got the Dominant panel on my side."

The feather moved from her bound knees and slowly made its way between her legs. The delicate touch of it drove her wild. She squirmed in pleasure as the feather touched her mound. Then Brie stopped breathing, waiting for his lips. When she felt his warm breath on her sex, she whimpered. His lips barely brushed her swollen clit before he settled back beside her.

Brie's whole body shuddered with need.

"I've taken each class, worked through each practicum with only one focus."

The feather stroked the side of her face, landing on her lips and tickling them until she laughed. His lips silenced her giggles. He kissed with such passion, such intensity that she froze.

The sounds of the other couples copulating filled the

room. Todd pulled away and moved his lips to her ear, whispering, "I will not take you tonight. I want your body to open of its own will, not just because I command it."

He began gently unwinding the ties. Then he removed the blindfold and brought her arms back over her head. He unlocked the thin silver cuff and kissed the inside of each wrist before placing them on her stomach.

She looked up into his crystal eyes, not knowing who this man was. "Thank you, Faelan."

"Anytime, blossom."

After the three Doms had left the room, Sir began the discussion with the Dominant trainers still in attendance.

"We would all like to hear your honest opinions of your Doms' performances." He turned to Lea first. "Ms. Taylor, how would you rate Master Allen's scene with you?"

Out of the corner of her eye, Brie saw Lea look up and smile. "Master Allen really seemed to care, Sir. He continually asked my color, eased up when I indicated that I was reaching yellow but did not stop. He pushed me like a good Dom should. I enjoyed the session with him."

"On a scale of one to ten, what would you rate him?" Master Coen asked.

She said without hesitation, "I would give him a six."

A well-built, bald trainer from the other table spoke up. "What would you say is his major weakness, Ms. Taylor?"

She shifted in her spot, making Brie wonder if it was difficult for her to answer. "I didn't feel like he was reading me as we went. He was so dependent on asking my color that he didn't notice what should have been obvious."

The female trainer at the table replied, "I concur with the submissive. Master Allen was oblivious to her discomfort until he asked."

"Thank you for your observations, Ms. Taylor," Sir said. "You may kneel."

Lea immediately settled on the floor in a graceful motion.

Sir addressed Mary next. "Give us your assessment of Mr. Hall's performance, Miss Wilson."

Mary answered, "He still has a lot to learn, Sir. The cautious way he used the crop was a complete turn-off. He might as well have hit me with a wet noodle."

The silence in the room was deafening.

Sir replied with ice in his voice, "Miss Wilson, a respectful evaluation is expected of a submissive. Demeaning your Dom's performance is neither welcomed nor appropriate."

Brie felt a chill run through her bones, even though she was not the one being corrected.

Mary answered meekly, "Sorry, Sir."

"Reword your statement," Marquis Gray instructed, his face expressionless.

Mary took a deep breath before starting again. "Lord Hall was not confident with his use of the crop."

The bald trainer at the other table interjected, "I believe some of the fault lies with you, Miss Wilson. I noticed you were emotionally unreadable, which made you difficult to work with. It surprises me, considering the extensive training you've received at this school."

Brie shuddered at the trainer's assessment of Mary. She had never thought that by evaluating the training Doms, they might end up inviting negative comments from the Dominant trainers themselves. However, she realized she had been foolish to think otherwise. As submissives, they were always under scrutiny—always.

Ms. Clark challenged Mary by asking, "You started with his weakness, but I would like to know his strengths."

Mary took quite a while to answer. "He was…good-looking and pounded me decently."

All eight trainers stared at her without comment.

Mary was failing miserably with her evaluation, so Sir mercifully cut it short. "What would you rate him?"

"A three, maybe four."

"Since I find your evaluation a waste of our time," Sir stated, "kneel down and rethink your answers. We will speak after class."

Mary sank to the floor slowly.

"Miss Bennett," Sir began, his voice tainted with irritation. Although she knew it wasn't directed at her, Brie still felt a quelling of her spirit. "How would you evaluate your Dom's performance?"

"Sir, I would rate Faelan a seven."

The brawny trainer from the other team jumped on her statement. "Why so high? Explain yourself."

"I know it may seem odd, considering we did not have intercourse, but it was that very fact that set him apart." Brie braved a look at the Dominant trainer. "I'm not sure how well I would have handled a more intimate encounter because I'm acquainted with Faelan outside of class. The fact he chose to tease rather than conquer me was shrewd. It left me craving another session with him."

Ms. Clark asked, "Had he demanded intercourse, would you have complied?"

"Of course," Brie answered, remembering to keep her eyes lowered when she answered the Dominatrix. "However, it would have been out of obedience, not personal desire."

Brie heard the woman trainer at the other table remark, "I did find his choice of scene odd, but it makes sense now."

"Miss Bennett." Brie looked up, and a distinguished white-haired gentleman nodded to her. "What do you see as a weakness of Mr. Wallace?"

She answered with apprehension, "Although Faelan read me well throughout the scene, he did come across a little overconfident."

Brie saw the female trainer smile. The fourth man, a striking Native American, replied, "A valid point." Brie had presumed the bald man was the leader of the panel, but the authoritative way this Dom spoke said differently. He glanced over to Sir. "I think we have what we need from your submissives."

Sir ordered Brie to kneel. She followed his command as all of the Dominant trainers got up from their table and left the room. Sir followed them out and spoke to the head trainer in the hallway for several minutes.

It allowed Brie time to reflect on the scene with Faelan. It shocked her that through that short encounter, Blue Eyes had accomplished the one thing she did not want. The light caress of his feather still lingered on her skin, causing goose bumps of desire for the boy.

A New Kind of Clubbing

B rie had a fitful sleep that night. Her heart was being pulled in too many directions and that played out in her dreams. Tono ripped the sash from his kimono and wrapped it over her eyes while Faelan restrained her in chains, but on the sidelines the buzzing sound of Marquis Gray's violet wand all but drowned out Sir's command for her. She woke up drenched in sweat, crying out a name, but unable to recall which man's name had been on her lips.

Why? Why did Blue Eyes have to complicate things even further?

Brie couldn't go back to sleep, so she pulled out her laptop and looked up the meaning of Faelan. She read that it was an old Irish word meaning 'young wolf'. The boy was pursuing her like a single-minded predator, but he hadn't jumped her like a mindless beast. No, he was drawing her in by denying her—*clever boy.*

The next day, Brie asked Mr. Reynolds if she could leave an hour early. He seemed to be in an especially chipper mood and gave her the afternoon off. She took the extra time to soak in the tub, cover herself in silky lotion and work on her hair, makeup and nails. She made sure everything was perfect, down to the minutest detail. It was important to Brie to make a good impression on her new community.

Brie pulled up to The Haven and saw Mary standing outside, next to the five trainers. She was surprised and a little disappointed not to see Tono in attendance as well. She had naturally assumed, because of his mastery of Kinbaku, that he would be part of the outing. She wondered if he was already inside, showcasing his talents. Even if she didn't get the chance to work with him tonight, just seeing him would do her heart good… *Or maybe not.* Could she really handle watching another sub enjoy his gift of the rope?

She left her long coat in the car, letting out a nervous sigh before locking it. The place looked like a trendy nightclub, complete with neon lights. Couples passed by as she made her way to the group—men in dark shirts and jeans with duffle bags over their shoulders and women in fuck-me shoes, collars, vinyl outfits or extremely short skirts.

Brie suddenly found herself praying that Tono was *not* inside. She realized she could not handle seeing him harmonize with someone else, and that new revelation disturbed her. What did it mean? She walked over to Mary and stood beside her, unable to hide the unease she felt.

Naturally, Sir noticed and commented. "Are you ready for tonight, Miss Bennett? Unlike most clubs, this one allows for sexual interaction."

She looked him in the eyes and melted, all other concerns instantly forgotten. "I'm looking forward to mingling with the local D/s community, Sir."

Master Coen spoke up. "Actually, Miss Bennett, you will not be mingling. You are only here to observe and perform."

Brie felt a warm tingling in her loins when he said the word 'perform'. What would it be like and who would she be partnered with? Possibly Sir? The anticipation heightened her sense of arousal.

Lea had shown up during the short exchange. The three girls were given strict instructions to remain at the sides of their trainers and to observe only. Sir paired up each student with a trainer, giving Brie to Master Anderson. She had to swallow her disappointment.

Master Anderson held out his arm to her. Brie looked up into his intense green eyes and was surprised by the thrill of connection she felt. He definitely had that commanding Dom quality she adored, but Brie knew so little about the man. She assumed the connection was due to him being good friends with Sir, which made Master Anderson a conduit of sorts. Being with him was a little like being with Sir.

Brie held her breath as they walked through the doors, curious as to what she would find on the other side. She was surprised to see that it looked similar to a normal club, with a large gathering area in the middle full of people milling about. Her idea of a dark dungeon with the screams of submissives filling the air was not a reality for this stylish venue.

It wasn't until she looked to the right that she saw

the real entertainment. Along the peripheral walls were numerous alcoves. Each one seemed to have its own theme and equipment. The one closest to her had a spanking horse. It was a padded bench with side rails so that the submissive could sit comfortably and remain still during the session. The girl lying down on the bench had on scarlet vinyl pants with the ass cheeks cut out, leaving the exposed skin open for punishment. The Dom behind her was spanking her with a large wooden paddle. Her moans of pleasure echoed in the room, joining the cries of several others.

Brie felt a gush of wetness between her legs in response to their passionate reactions. This was so her kind of place!

Master Anderson broke from the group and led Brie around to each scene, adding commentary from time to time. "Do you see the way she is anticipating each stroke of the cane and moving slightly just before it hits? The Dom should really correct her. It's only showcasing his inexperience and ruining the scene." Before they moved to the next alcove, Brie caught a whiff of a fragrance she instantly identified as sandalwood. She wondered where it was coming from.

When they stepped closer to the next scene, she noticed a pleasant trace of musk. The alcove itself had an impressive St. Andrew's cross made of smoky glass with black leather cuffs. The aroma seemed the perfect complement to the environment.

The man bound to the cross was enduring the focused attention of his Mistress, who was teasing his cock with electricity. The man's guttural cries sent a shiver through Brie. There was no doubt he was turned on, based on the rigidness of his member.

Master Anderson squeezed her hand and moved her on to the next scene. He had to part the crowd that had gathered so Brie could see what was happening.

The scent of jasmine filled Brie's nostrils, adding to the visual of three brown-haired subs kneeling on the ground, attached together by a string of nipple clamps on a chain. She had never seen anything like it and found the scene erotic, although she knew from personal experience that nipple clamps hurt.

The Dom went to the first girl and allowed her to suck his cock while the two others watched. His hand combed through her short hair and he said something to her that made her smile with his cock still in her mouth. He pulled away from her and went to the middle girl. He guided his shaft into her mouth and commanded that the other two play with his balls while he face-fucked her.

Brie looked down at the floor, overcome with desire.

"Do you like what you see, my young Miss Bennett?"

She made sure to speak loudly enough for him to hear without disturbing the scene. "Yes, Master Anderson."

He leaned down and told her, "Tonight you shall address me as Master."

Brie braved a look into his luminous green eyes, realizing that he was more than a trainer tonight; he was to be her partner. She answered quietly, "Yes, Master."

Master Anderson smiled mischievously when he asked, "Can you guess what my specialty is?"

She stared up at the towering Dom, at a loss for

words, so she just shook her head in response.

"I am the master of the bullwhip. Have you ever felt its bite?"

Again, Brie shook her head, afraid to speak. The bullwhip was a far more intimidating appliance than any flogger.

"Do not fret, Miss Bennett. I can whip you with the lightest of touches." He lightly brushed a fingertip against her arm. "Or cut you deep with a quick snap of my wrist." He said it matter-of-factly, without malicious intent.

Brie let out a nervous sigh. "I look forward to feeling your expertise, Master."

His laughter was low and engaging. "I like your enthusiasm, young Brie. It contrasts so well with the look of apprehension showing on your face."

Master Anderson led her to an especially long and empty alcove, ripe with the clean scent of an ocean breeze, which made perfect sense as the inside walls were painted a calming blue. It contrasted sharply with the chains hanging from the ceiling.

"Our time has come, Miss Bennett."

Brie's loins contracted in…what? Fear or excitement? She wasn't sure. She bowed to him and answered dutifully, "Yes, Master."

"You will remove all your clothes, except for your skirt."

She quickly undressed to his specifications, but squeaked unconsciously when she saw Sir hand Master Anderson a fierce-looking leather whip, the kind Indiana Jones used. It looked far, far more menacing than

Marquis' flogger. Brie put on a brave face, knowing that Sir was going to observe the scene. To calm herself, she focused on keeping her body supple and pleasing while she waited for the next order.

"Very good, slave. Move over to the X on the floor and face the wall. Put your feet on either side of it. It will be the stance you remain in for the entire scene."

"Yes, Master." Brie trembled when he took her left wrist and lifted it high, then buckled it into the leather cuff attached to the chain.

She could feel the eyes of others on her and sensed a crowd gathering. Master Anderson took her right arm and fastened it tightly. Then he pulled on the chain, spreading her arms out wider and making it taut. She swayed as he adjusted it, but did not move from her designated spot.

He leaned down next to her ear. "We will use the common safe words. I normally use a different phrase, but the rules of this establishment don't allow for it. A simple 'red' will end our session, although I do not expect you will use it." He moved to her other ear. "I plan to make you drip for me, slave." He moved her long, brown hair to the front, covering her breasts and exposing her back. Then his warm lips landed on her neck and he sucked on the sensitive skin until it burned. Brie moaned softly as he pulled away, her whole body tingling from the contact.

He said from behind her, "I am going to warm up first. Listen to the crack of the whip and know that it will soon be caressing your skin."

Brie jumped, her heart skipping a beat the first time

the whip cracked beside her head and she felt the rush of air. Her nipples hardened into tight buds.

"You're lucky you landed in the same spot, slave. But I will punish you next time, for I commanded that you *must not* move." She could hear the amusement in his voice. He had obviously known she would jump.

She took a deep breath to calm her nerves and answered, "I will not move, Master."

The whip cracked on the other side. It came with incredible speed and the sound of it hurt her ears. Brie twitched, but didn't budge from her spot. Surprisingly, her pussy pulsed in response. Her time with Marquis had accustomed her body to the idea that pleasure could be found in pain.

"Are you ready, slave?"

Brie closed her eyes and said in a barely audible whisper, "Yes, Master."

The first stroke landed and felt like a warm touch, nothing more. Brie opened her eyes in shock. She heard Master Anderson chuckle softly. "Were you expecting something different, slave?"

"Yes, Master."

"Keep still as I warm up that lovely back of yours."

The large whip came down on her over and over again, licking and warming her skin. It was exciting and sensual, while at the same time looking dramatic and painful. Brie loved it and wondered if the crowd was amazed at her brave silence.

"And now, slave, you will earn your stripes."

Brie's heart stuck in her throat. A whimper escaped her lips and was not lost on her Master.

"Is your heart racing? Good… I want you to count as I stroke your back. A set of six to start."

Brie yelped when the first landed on her skin, leaving a burning heat in its path. "One," she finally remembered to call out.

"Color, slave?"

Brie took a deep breath before answering. "Green."

She heard the snap as the next licked her skin, higher up her back. It stung and a groan escaped her lips before she uttered, "Two."

He did not wait, lashing her a third time. "Three." She gulped, debating whether to cry and let the pain release in the tears, or remain tearless and brave.

The fourth lashed across in the other direction, taking her by surprise and causing her to choke on her shriek. She knew he was waiting, so she called out, "Four."

"You are a gutsy slave. I did not expect you to take it quietly."

His compliment cemented her determination not to cry *or* scream. She took the next two lashes while breathing deeply, letting the tail of the whip reverberate on her skin, much as she had during her session with the cane.

"It seems you need it a little harder, slave."

Brie's whole body tensed as she suddenly realized her choice to be silent was sending him the wrong message. *Will I ever learn?*

He walked over to her and rested his chin on her shoulder. "Don't worry, little one. I know you are at your limit. I want to challenge you with two more that will bite. What is the point of taking the whip if you aren't going to experience all of its character? However, I leave it up to you."

Brie took several calming breaths while she thought about his offer. Master Anderson was right—she wanted to experience it all, even though she was uncertain if she could endure it.

"Hold on to the fact you are almost done. Only two more, slave, and then you will wear the proud marks of your fearless spirit."

His words infused her with courage. Hadn't she promised herself not to be afraid of things she hadn't tried? "I will take two more, Master, if it pleases you."

"Remember, as always, it only takes one word to set you free," he murmured, kissing her neck before moving back into position.

Yes, she was the one in power. This was *her* choice.

Master Anderson announced to the crowd, "I want you to count this time."

Brie imagined him winding up for the first stroke, and then she heard the whip of the tail just before it slashed across her back. Brie cried out from the biting pain while the crowd enthusiastically shouted, "One!"

"Color, slave?"

She felt a welt growing on her back in response to the wicked sting. "Yellow," she panted. The chains moved in harmony with her quivering body.

"One more. Do not tense, slave. Accept this gift."

"Yes, Master."

Brie closed her eyes and breathed out slowly. This was the last one, and she wanted to experience every nuance of it. Time slowed down as the implement of her pleasure-pain raced to connect with her skin. It landed across her back—a burning, piercing pain that warmed the entire area, setting it on fire.

She directed that feeling to course through her body, forcing it to travel to her loins and concentrate there. It was her transformative abilities that took his gift of the whip and turned it into something wild and beautiful within her.

"Two!" she heard the crowd yell.

She swayed on the chain, focusing all her attention on the fire in her loins. Brie felt his hands on her as he undid the binding of one wrist and then the other. He held her in place and asked, "Have you flown too far into subspace to please me?"

She laid her head against his torso. "No, Master. I need to please you."

"Present yourself, then," he commanded.

Brie gratefully dropped to the floor and opened her legs to him, *needing* the fire inside to explode in release.

She looked behind her lustfully and was stunned to see that Master Anderson had a cock that almost rivaled Boa's. He pushed against her opening with little resistance. Her body welcomed him, craving his attention. She heard his groan of satisfaction as her body took the length and girth of his manhood. He began pumping into her, and she met each stroke, crying out in abandon. The high of subspace made each thrust pure paradise.

It didn't take long for his immense cock to bring her over the edge. Brie strained against him as her orgasm peaked and then detonated. She screamed as her inner muscles tensed around his large member, squeezing rhythmically in their own sexual song.

He responded by shooting his essence deep inside her. Thrust after passionate thrust bathed her insides with his maleness. Afterwards, he wrapped his arm around her and kissed the welts on her back tenderly. "Well earned, young slave."

He disengaged, then gathered her into his arms and carried her to a chair in the corner of the alcove. He held her to his chest and rocked her gently. She snuggled into his chest and closed her eyes, forgetting the crowd. The scent of the ocean filled her mind and soothed her spirit.

"You are remarkable," he told her, playing with her long, brown curls. "Few subs demonstrate that level of curiosity and confidence so early on."

"Thank you, Master."

He continued to stroke her hair without saying any more. She took a brief peek at the crowd and saw many had left, but she caught Sir's eye. For an instant, she recognized that look he'd had before, when she'd been in Marquis Gray's arms, but it disappeared and the authoritative headmaster returned. He nodded to her and turned to talk to Ms. Clark.

Master Anderson commanded Brie to wipe the floor clean of their sweat and lovemaking while he disinfected the cuffs. Then he rubbed the tail of his whip with special cleaner, rolled it up and placed it in a bag. He tossed Brie's clothes in her direction, but put her corset in his bag. He winked at her. "You do *not* want to wear a corset after a bullwhipping. Besides, I want you to show off your back tonight. You did well and deserve the attention."

He held his hand out to Brie and walked her over to Sir after she took it. "I have a demonstration in fifteen minutes, Thane. I hand her over to your care."

Sir held out his arm to Brie, and she clasped on to it

eagerly. The fact she was half-naked only enhanced her feeling of connection to him. He walked her slowly to the next alcove so she could witness the play.

Brie was surprised to see Mary tied to a pole. The sound of Mozart filled the alcove as Marquis Gray worked his magic with the flogger. Instead of cries, Mary belted out peals of laughter. What was escaping from her lips was the sound of pure joy.

Brie felt tears prick her eyes. *I'm happy for you, Mary…*

Sir pulled her away from the scene and asked, "So, what did you think of Master Anderson's skill?"

She was thankful for his question, because it gave her the right to look him in the eye. "It was a unique experience, Sir. I can't believe he can make it feel so light and pleasant."

"And what did you think of its bite?"

"I…" Brie became lost in his captivating gaze and had to force herself to speak. "I am glad I tried it, Sir. However…"

"What?" he encouraged.

Brie was unsure if her answer would displease him. "I would only choose to do it on rare occasions…when it pleases my Master."

"The bullwhip does not call to you, then?"

"No, Sir."

He patted her hand gently as he guided her on to a new scene, but every fiber of her being was focused on his touch and she was unaware of anyone or anything else. It wasn't until Sir squeezed her hand that she took notice of the girl standing in front of her.

"You have an admirer who wishes to speak, Brie."

A young sub with large, doe-like eyes, who was

dressed in a black vinyl corset and skirt, was standing in front of her. "I just wanted to say how impressed I was at how you handled your Master's whip. You've inspired me."

Brie smiled in embarrassment and looked down at the floor. She grasped at the only thing that came to mind. "A wise Master once told me to follow my instincts. It helps me to open up to new experiences when I'm hesitant."

The young girl bowed and said sweetly, "Thank you."

Brie crushed her face against Sir's shoulder when the young girl had left.

He chuckled. "What's wrong, Brie? Can't handle having a sub groupie?"

She groaned into his shirt.

He added, "A wise Master, huh? I prefer to be called intelligent, quick-witted, experienced. Wise…that's for old men."

She smiled up at him. "Sir, you are wise beyond your years."

He patted her hand again without speaking as he walked her towards the next scene. Brie purred inside, loving this rare chance to connect. She wanted to ask him a thousand questions but stood beside him quietly, hoping he would open up.

The scene playing out in front of them consisted of three performers—a large, leather-clad Dom and two naked females. The redhead's wrists were bound to the ankles of the blonde. She enthusiastically lapped the blonde's bare mound while the Dom fucked her with an enormous glass dildo.

Sir grunted softly. "The overabundant use of toys remains a mystery to me. I understand the visual effect for the audience, but wielding a dildo is never as satisfying as using your God-given instrument."

Brie wanted to tell him that he had the most perfect God-given instrument known to man. Instead, she replied, "I appreciate your perspective, Sir."

"It is understandable that Doms and subs alike crave the newest toy, the latest fad, or the edgiest play, but in the end it comes down to a couple exploring their innermost fears and desires. The bells and whistles are really just for show. It's the inner struggles and personal triumphs others can't see that mark a successful D/s relationship."

"I agree, Sir. I want to be stretched and honed all my life. I desire someone who will challenge my fears and make me confront my hidden desires, especially those I don't even know exist yet."

Sir chuckled lightly. "You will either be a Dom's fantasy or his greatest challenge, Brie."

She almost blurted, "What am I to you, Sir?" but thankfully her lips remained shut. It was too personal. She didn't want to say or do anything that might ruin this time with him.

An unfamiliar Dom came up to Sir and asked to speak with him. They moved over to the social area and Brie stood silently by as the two men discussed the finer points of clitoral stimulation. She didn't mind. In fact, she was proud to stand half-naked beside Sir, listening to the prudent advice he gave. She imagined other submissives walking past, admiring her red badges of courage as well as her handsome Dom, and it tickled her heart.

Auction Day: Mystery Dom

B rie had no idea who would win her for the fourth auction, or what to expect, since Mr. Gallant hadn't assigned them to write in their journals that week. The girls gathered together with the normal sense of excitement just before it was to begin. Auction Days were always exhilarating. The sense of ownership and the thrill of the unknown were an unbeatable combination.

"You two are going to meet me afterwards, right?" Brie asked.

"Sorry, can't," Mary answered.

"Me neither, Brie," Lea said. "My mother is coming into town for the week and I have to get things ready. I'm going to have to tell her about this course and I am a little scared, but I don't really have a choice with these nightly classes."

Brie gave her a squeeze. "Good luck with that, friend. I don't envy you. However, I insist that we get together, even if it's just for an hour tomorrow."

"Well, if you are willing to meet near my apartment, we could go out for coffee or something," Lea suggested.

Brie turned to Mary. "Will that work for you?"

"Sure, whatever. At least you aren't going to try to point that damn camera at my face."

Brie momentarily toyed with the idea of bringing it, just to bug her. "So, we're agreed. Meet at Starbucks next to Lea's place at noon. We can share our experiences then."

"Sounds like a plan," Lea said, pointing towards the left discreetly. Brie turned and saw Ms. Clark approaching.

"Miss Bennett, you will be first, then Miss Wilson, followed by Ms. Taylor. We have an unusual request for this one. A member of the audience has requested that Miss Bennett wear a blindfold before bidding begins." The trainer whipped one out and proceeded to tie it around her head, a little too tightly for Brie's liking.

Ms. Clark whispered, "He must have read about your weakness, Miss Bennett. I wouldn't be surprised if you are thoroughly tested and punished today. I suggest you keep your eyes glued to the floor if you want the ability to sit by the end of the evening." She said it with relish, as if she hoped Brie would fail and suffer greatly. The woman loved to be right, especially if it meant Brie was wrong.

Ms. Clark took her by the hand and led her onto the stage. Brie held her head at a respectful angle and placed her hands at her sides, open and relaxed. Despite the unusual circumstance, she would not let this get to her.

"Miss Bennett is twenty-two, with a bachelor's degree in filmmaking outside these walls. Her trainers describe her as dedicated but undisciplined." Brie forced her jaw not to drop. *Undisciplined?* That was such an insult!

"Being that this is our fourth auction, we will begin the bidding at four hundred," the auctioneer stated. Brie was gratified that the bidding reached a thousand dollars before it ended. "Going once… Going twice… Sold to the man in the front."

Brie was confused. Normally the name of the Dom was announced, but even that was being hidden from her. For a brief second, she thought someone she cared for had won her bid, but the minute the Dom touched her arm Brie's hopes were dashed. She didn't recognize his touch or his scent, which was a deep musk. As he led her off the stage, she was more curious than ever as to why he had gone to all this trouble to conceal himself.

She waited patiently, listening as Mary was won by a Master named Regal and Lea went to a man named Sire Luke. When Sir ended the auction, her Dom led her down the hallway. Brie walked beside her mystery Dom, wondering at his silence.

He guided her into a room and she heard the door shut behind her. Brie sensed that she was alone. She stood there with butterflies in her stomach, excited by the intrigue. She was enjoying this game her Dom was playing. "Master?" she whispered, to double-check that she was indeed alone.

When no one answered, she slowly untied the blindfold, assuming that it was allowed because she hadn't been given a command otherwise. Before her was a black dress laid out on a table, along with a sexy garter belt and pair of hose, a pair of classy high heels and a single rose. There was also a card that read, 'Open Me'.

Brie picked it up and eagerly read her instructions: *Dress, put the flower in your hair, and get into the cab waiting for you. Enter the establishment and wait for me at the bar.*

She put the card down and immediately began to follow her mystery Dom's commands. The dress was a short lace number that perfectly matched the silk hose and black garter belt, but she noticed there were no panties included. She strapped on her high heels, broke the stem of the rose and tucked the flower behind her ear.

Brie left the room and walked down the empty hallway. It seemed strange to be going to an unknown destination to meet a Dom she hadn't seen. She walked up to the cab and got in, smoothing her dress several times in her excitement. What a charming way to start Auction Day!

She tried to give the cabbie a tip when he pulled up to the swanky hotel, but he assured her it had already been taken care of. She thanked him, then entered the hotel and made her way to the bar. Brie looked around, but only saw a group of older men watching sports on the screen at the bar. She walked to the other end and sat down on a stool to wait. The bartender came up and asked, "Miss Bennett?"

"Yes…" she answered in surprise.

He slid a small box over to her. "This is for you, as well as this drink." He placed a gin martini in front of her and left her alone.

Brie opened the box and found a silver chain inside.

Underneath was another note. *Put this bracelet on, knowing that it signifies your acceptance of the chain that binds you to me.*

She bit her lip in anticipation as she opened the clasp and put the chain around her wrist. Then she took a sip of the slightly dirty martini—it was perfection. She sighed nervously and looked around, wondering when he would show.

Ten minutes later, a man with deliciously long, black hair came up to her. He looked her over approvingly and gave her a wink. "The flower is a nice touch."

Brie hadn't expected her Dom to look like a rock star. She was unsure what to call him since his name had not been stated at the auction, so she fingered the rose lightly and said, "It *is* beautiful, thank you."

He smiled and ordered her another drink when she finished. "This isn't my normal mode of operation," he explained.

She had to assume that this was his first auction, which explained the odd way it had been handled. "Then I am honored." She looked at him curiously and asked, "What should I call you?"

He broke out in an all-out grin. "Raven will suffice. You ready to blow this joint?"

She smiled shyly. "If it pleases you, Raven."

"Don't bother finishing that drink." He stood up and gestured towards the door.

Brie picked up her purse and was about to get off the stool when she felt a firm hand on her shoulder. "Remain seated."

Brie trembled at the sound of his voice.

Raven immediately responded, "Hey, look, buddy.

You get your hands off the girl. She's coming with me."

The voice behind her answered, "No, she is not. Ask her."

Raven squared his jaw angrily and told Brie, "Give me the word and I'll be happy to deck this guy."

Brie quickly realized her mistake and stammered, "I'm sorry, Raven…" She formulated a viable excuse in her head to explain her mistake. "You see, this man is my blind date."

"The freak is your date?" Raven asked incredulously.

A shiver went down Brie's spine as she wondered just whom it was who held her so firmly. "It would be best if you leave now," she answered.

The voice behind her stated, "I concur. Your presence is not welcome. Please leave."

Raven cocked his head at Brie. "You can't be serious. You'd rather go out with this sideshow act than me?"

Brie looked down at the floor, ignoring him.

Her Dom stated, "We will leave."

He guided her off the stool and walked her out of the bar. Brie turned to see the bartender silencing Raven before he could cause a scene.

"I'm sorry. I thought he…" Brie began.

"I found it amusing, or I wouldn't have let it continue." Her Dom stopped and turned Brie to face him. "Look at me," he commanded.

Brie let her gaze trail up his torso, noting the expensive business suit and his striped tie before her eyes beheld his face. His sandy hair was cut military-style, but what demanded her attention was the fact that her Master's right cheek was caved in and a patch covered his eye. Before she could respond, he said, "Injury. You will not speak of it."

She nodded, focusing on his soft lips. Despite his facial deformity, he had kind lips. "What shall I call you?"

"What my men did. Captain."

"Yes, Captain."

He put his hand on her back and guided her towards the elevator. "The cretin was correct. The flower *is* a nice touch. You look lovely, pet."

"Thank you, Captain. The clothes are exquisite, as is the bracelet." She held up her wrist to admire it again.

"I like my pets to wear a reminder of their position."

"It is beautifully effective, Captain."

He walked her to the door of his room. "When you enter I want you to take off your shoes and stand by the bed." He swung the door open and ushered her inside.

Brie followed his command, wondering with trepidation what he had in mind when she saw the chain attached to the bedpost.

He came up behind her and unzipped the dress, then let it slip slowly to the floor. Then he unfastened her bra and tossed it aside. He caressed her breasts, playing with and tugging on her nipples until he'd made her drip with need for him.

Captain kissed her shoulder lightly before kneeling and attaching the metal cuff to her ankle. He stood up and informed Brie, "You will remain chained to the bed for the duration of our time together."

She gazed at his face, wanting to say something but knowing it was not her right. He unbuttoned his shirt and tossed it on a chair. She noticed numerous scars over his chest, probably caused by shrapnel. She felt an overwhelming sense of compassion and blurted without thinking, "May I kiss them, Captain?"

The indignant look on his face made her cringe. He said nothing, but moved to an overstuffed lounge chair and sat down. He looked at her dismissively. "You should know that I wanted the blonde, but my friend insisted you would be a better fit."

Brie knew she had offended him and accepted his insult. "With all due respect, Captain, I have found that the outer shell doesn't matter much."

He shook his head with a bemused look. "Touché." He patted his knee and commanded, "Kneel at my feet, pet."

The chain rattled as she moved towards him. It was long enough for her to accommodate his wishes. She knelt beside him and he began stroking her hair. She closed her eyes and savored the feel of his fingers running through her long curls. He spent a considerable amount of time petting her hair in silence. Eventually, however, he stopped and she heard him unzip his pants.

"Suck my cock, pet."

Brie moved between his legs and grasped his hard shaft. She wrapped her lips around him and slowly took the length of his manhood into her mouth.

"I like it slow and gentle."

She moaned in response and moved her hair out of the way so he could watch her pink lips go down on his maleness. He shifted into a more relaxed position and let her work his cock for what seemed like an hour. She'd never taken that long to love a man's shaft. Heck, she'd never had a man last that long before. By the time he ordered her to sit on his lap, her mouth and tongue were sore from her concentrated effort to please him.

Brie crawled onto his lap to the clinking sound of the chain. He slid her pussy down over his hard shaft, pushing himself deep into her, then instructed her not to move. "Look at me, pet."

She stared into his good eye and smiled warmly. It didn't matter that he was disfigured; the man had a gentle soul. But she could tell he needed something more from her, so she moved her hands behind his head to undo the ties of his patch. "May I, Captain?"

He stiffened and she wondered if she'd overstepped her bounds again, but to her relief he answered quietly, "Yes."

Brie slowly undid the ties and removed the patch from his face. Underneath was a sunken eyelid, healed shut. She leaned over and kissed it lightly.

She heard his intake of breath as he grabbed her hips and his shaft started pulsating inside her. He threw his head back and groaned softly. When his orgasm had subsided, he looked at her questioningly, cradling her cheek in his hand. "Why did you do that, pet?"

"I needed to, Captain. Thank you."

He slowly lifted her off his cock and told her to kneel beside him again. She felt sensuous in her black garter belt and hose, resting her head on his lap while Captain stroked her hair. There was such an aching need radiating from her Dom—Brie desperately hoped she could meet it.

A short time later, she heard a knock at the door. He stopped the petting and stood up to answer it. "Stay," he ordered quietly as he quickly got dressed.

He walked to the door and told the hotel staff, "There is no need to come in. Thank you."

She heard the door shut and then the clatter of a cart as he rolled it in her direction. "I have dinner, pet." He placed a plate of food and a silver bowl on the coffee table in front of her.

She noticed there was only one plate and wondered if she would be expected to watch him eat. Her stomach grumbled against her will and she bowed her head in shame.

Captain sat back down and fingered her curls, chuckling under his breath. He leaned over and cut off a small piece of meat, then brought the fork to her lips. She opened her mouth and slid her teeth against the tines, moaning in pleasure when she tasted the tender morsel.

"Good, girl."

He cut himself a slightly larger piece and chewed it. Even though Brie felt like a dog, there was something comforting about kneeling beside him, being fed by her Dom. He made her feel cared for by taking turns and cutting smaller pieces so that she could eat gracefully.

"Thank you, Captain," she said, looking up at him.

"My pleasure, pet."

When he'd finished the meal, he put the bowl down on the floor and filled it with water. "Drink. Be sure to lift your ass in the air and look at me lustfully while you lap it up."

Brie turned to face him, liking the sound of the jangling chain as she moved. It gave her a feeling of possession. She looked at her injured Master as she sensually lapped the water. Yes, she was acting the part of a dog, but she made sure she was the sexiest damn dog he'd ever seen.

"That's nice, pet," he complimented, rubbing his hand against his crotch. She watched the outline of his shaft grow under his ministration. When his dick began straining against his slacks, he stood up and removed them.

He picked up the bowl and placed it back on the coffee table before commanding, "On the bed, now. Present yourself."

Brie quickly got off the floor and made her way onto the large bed to the sound of the clattering chain. She arched her back alluringly, spreading herself open for his pleasure.

"You do have a beautiful cunt, pet. It appears hungry for what I can give it."

"It is, Captain. I am desperate for you."

Captain smiled as he climbed onto the bed and positioned himself between her legs. He ran his hands over her round buttocks, growling, "I do enjoy pleasing an obedient pet." Taking a fistful of hair, he pulled her head back and thrust the full length of his shaft into her in one solid stroke. She gasped in surprise.

"Am I too much for you, pet?"

"No…" she panted. "Just right, Captain."

"Good, because I plan to ride you long and hard." He let go of her hair and grabbed her hips.

The thrusts he gave her sent bursts of heat through her body and the whole room echoed with the sound of the frantically rattling chain.

"You know how to ride your pet," she complimented between gasps.

He grunted in response and pushed her flat onto the bed. "I want to hear you scream in pleasure." Captain squeezed her ass cheeks as he gave her everything he had.

Brie shrieked at the force of his passion, but then she met it and cried, "Oh, Captain… O Captain, my Captain!"

He slowed down momentarily to slap her ass and said drolly, "Cheeky little thing." She screamed lustfully when he went back to his unrestrained fucking of her. Unexpectedly, he stopped and collapsed on top of her, holding her tight. The stillness allowed her body to catch up and she felt the welcomed chills take over as her orgasm descended upon her.

"That's it. Caress your owner's shaft, you impish pet."

She groaned and squirmed underneath him as he worked over her body, bringing her past the edge over and over again. Hours later, his cock finally stiffened inside her with its own orgasmic dance and she purred in contentment. His pleasure was her pleasure.

Afterwards, he rolled over on his back, breathing heavily. Captain stared up at the ceiling, saying nothing as Brie curled up next to him. He automatically began stroking her hair again.

Finally, he broke the silence with a barely audible command. "You may lick them."

She smiled in gratitude as she got on all fours and tenderly ministered to each and every scar…

May I Humbly Suggest?

The next afternoon, Brie took the light rail to Lea's apartment to avoid traffic. She sat in the back of the train car, watching the constant stream of people enter and leave. It was entertaining because she made up stories in her head to go along with the people she observed, from the homeless bum (who was actually a millionaire trying to regain his humanity by denying himself) to the little grandma (who looked all proper with her perfect hairdo and conservative dress, but was actually a fierce Dominatrix who made grown men cry).

There was one couple, however, who caught Brie's attention without her needing to make up their story. It played out clearly in front of her, even though no one else seemed to notice. When they entered the car, the young man pushed his girl down onto an empty seat. To the average onlooker, it might have appeared the grungy youth was being kind and making sure his girl was seated, but the force he'd used and the way he was lording over her spoke only of one thing—a power play.

Brie tried to catch a glimpse of the girl, not wanting

to come off like a nosy onlooker. The young woman had an extremely thin frame and a despondent aura around her. Her watery eyes made it clear she was miserable.

Brie heard the man growl under his breath, "Do it."

The girl bowed her head lower, shaking it slowly.

The male stared at her in disgust. The girl cowered under his intense stare, wiping away the tears that escaped her tightly closed lids.

"Do it," he commanded again.

Her whole body shook in fear, but she did not move. "I'm *not* asking…"

Again, the girl shook her head.

The look on the man's face transformed from disgust to rage in the blink of an eye. His glare was so intense it looked as if it were burning into his girlfriend's skull. His voice was cool. "Understand there will be consequences."

Brie noticed the girl shudder in response before she looked up at him pleadingly. Brie was not surprised to see the collar around her gaunt neck, confirming her initial suspicion. "I'm sorry," the sub squeaked.

"Don't," he said, turning away from her. "Apologies mean nothing."

More tears fell down her cheeks, but the sub said no more, apparently accepting her fate.

The man glanced over in Brie's direction and she quickly averted her eyes, trying to hide the abhorrence she felt. She knew there were submissives who enjoyed humiliation in public, but it was disturbingly obvious that this was not the case for the girl seated across the aisle.

The man snarled in a low voice, "You have one more chance."

The girl turned her face towards him, and that was when Brie saw the bruise on her cheek. "I can't," she whimpered.

Chills traveled down Brie's spine. This was not a power play between a Dom and his sub. This was an abusive Dom wannabe taking advantage of an inexperienced submissive.

Brie popped out of her seat and approached them. She knew the protocol needed to appease the male, so she turned to him first, trying to keep her tone respectful. "Sir, may I speak with her?"

"Who the hell are you?" he barked.

She could not meet his hateful gaze when she answered, but kept her eyes cast downward in seeming reverence. "I'm no one, sir. But I have a humble suggestion for your girlfriend with the lovely collar."

He snorted, as though he understood that she recognized their D/s relationship. He seemed to stand a little prouder when he answered, "Fine, you may speak."

Brie gracefully knelt beside the wretched girl and smiled tenderly. "Hi, my name is Brie. What's yours?"

The girl looked up at her 'Dom' and waited for his nod before she replied softly. "Candy. My name is Candy."

"That's a good name. You look perfectly delicious." Brie saw the slightest glimmer in the girl's eye, and it suddenly dawned on her what to do. She dug through her purse and pulled out her wallet, then took out the business card Sir had given her. It was something she cherished, but Brie knew with certainty that this girl needed it more.

She handed it over, saying, "May I humbly suggest this course? It's changed my life."

Before the girl could read it, the man grabbed it from her. "What's this?" He laughed unkindly. "Yes, this is exactly what *you* need," he said, giving the card back.

Brie put her hand on Candy's trembling knee. "Trust me. This will change your life for the better."

The 'Dom' addressed Brie, so she stood up and turned towards him. He dared to grab her chin to look her over. "You *are* a lovely thing. Come with us, so I can see what you've learned at this Center of yours."

Brie pulled away from him, trying to hide the revulsion she felt, afraid that a misstep on her part would guarantee that Candy wouldn't be allowed to attend the Training Center. "I'm sorry, sir, but I cannot."

His eyes narrowed angrily—he was obviously unused to subs denying him. "Why?"

She caressed the collar around her neck when she answered in a whisper, "Only my Sir commands me."

The wannabe actually laughed. "Loyal, are you?" He turned to Candy and remarked, "You could learn a lot from this one. Maybe I'll let you take the class. You need it, because truth be told, you suck."

Brie backed away with her head down, muttering, "Thank you, sir." She returned to her seat and gazed out of the window. She smiled to herself, thrilled that she had been given the chance to pass on the information to a sub who truly needed it. Once Candy learned what was expected of a real Dom, she would leave that poor excuse for a man.

Later that night, Brie sent an email to Rachael Dunningham:

```
Dear Rachael,

Today I recommended the Training Center
to a sub that could really use it. If a
girl named Candy contacts you wanting
to join in the next few weeks, I do not
want money to be an issue. If she does
not qualify for a scholarship, I am
willing to act as her sponsor. Although
I do not have much, I can commit to
fifty dollars a month until I pay the
full amount.

Thank you,
Brie Bennett
```

She shut her laptop, then picked up her purse and fished out her wallet. She opened it forlornly and looked at the empty space that had once held Sir's card. Even though she missed its comforting presence, she knew the card was exactly where it belonged.

Brie settled into her bed and let out a pitiful whimper. There were only two weeks left… Two weeks to experience all the trainers had for her in the safety and refuge of the Center. Even more distressing was the fact that she only had a short time before she would choose which Dom she wanted to call Master permanently.

In the suffocating silence of night, Brie couldn't shut out the nagging feeling that her choice might not be based solely on her heart, but on the growth her chosen Dom could provide. She was stunned to find herself unsure which of the four men it would be.

The Thrill of Objectification

Brie wondered if it would be uncomfortable seeing Blue Eyes now that she knew him as Faelan. She walked up to the entrance of the Submissive Training Center in her fuck-me heels and saw him standing there, waiting for her, the same as he always had. He acted normally, opening the door and letting her pass with his familiar, "Good evening, Miss Bennett."

She couldn't help smiling as she walked through the door. "Thank you, Mr. Wallace."

Brie headed to class and sat there patiently waiting for her evaluation. Lea rushed into the classroom just as the bell rang. She barely made it to her seat before the ringing ended. The girls knew Mr. Gallant wasn't happy at her tardiness, but he said nothing and picked up their evaluations.

"Another exceptional week for you three. Again, I must caution you not to let these scores confuse you. There is much to learn in the next two weeks and none of you are as prepared as you think."

Mr. Gallant handed Lea hers first, with a slight frown

on his typically friendly face. It was just enough to act as punishment for cutting class so close. "An eight from Sire Luke. Apparently your oral skills are improving, Ms. Taylor. Keep up the good work."

He gave Mary her packet. "Also an eight, Miss Wilson. You *especially* should not let this go to your head. Note the areas of weakness. For you, they are a serious concern."

Mr. Gallant handed Brie her evaluation with a tender look in his eye. "You received a nine. Unheard of at this level, and I am sure only given because of the emotional aspect of your encounter. However, it is obvious you gave your Dom exactly what he needed. For that you should be commended, but understand that your level of experience should preclude you from a score as high as this."

"Yes, Mr. Gallant."

Brie took her evaluation and lightly kissed the packet before opening it. Captain had been a kind Master—so tender and yet deliciously demanding of her body. She eagerly read his comments: 'It is a rare sub who knows what her Master needs better than he does himself.' 'Agreeable, pleasing.' 'Trusted instincts in lieu of Master's wishes. In my case, exactly what I needed.' 'Truly a beauty in mind and spirit.'

A tear fell from her cheek onto the paper.

"Anything wrong, Miss Bennett?" Mr. Gallant asked.

She shook her head. "No, Mr. Gallant." She patted the packet tenderly when she answered him. "It was a special encounter."

"Very well. Although your Dom meant it as a compliment, I would heed his observation about letting your gut instincts get in the way of your duty."

Brie bowed her head. He was the second trainer to mention her dependency on her instincts. "I understand I still have a lot to learn, Mr. Gallant."

"I'm not suggesting you ignore your instincts, but do not rely on them."

Brie suddenly wondered if he was the one responsible for recommending her to Captain.

The next words out of his mouth startled and unnerved Brie. "We only have two more weeks before the end of the course, which means this is the last week you will be in this class together. Next week, you three will be split up so we can focus on your particular interests and talents."

Brie looked forlornly at Lea and Mary. *Our last week together?*

"Expect this week to be a challenge. Up to this point, the training has centered on you finding your limits. This week shall center on submitting your will to your Doms' various needs."

He turned to Mary and asked, "Miss Wilson, are you familiar with the term 'objectification'?"

"Is that when a sub acts like a footstool or something?"

His lips became a thin line. "That is a very simplified example. Objectification is the practice of using a person as a tool for one's own pleasure. The sub's needs, thoughts and wants are of no consequence."

He looked directly at Brie when he continued, "To the uneducated, it may appear uncaring and disrespectful.

154

However, it actually speaks to a higher level of trust and intimacy. The submissive willingly gives her body over to her Dom to be used as he pleases. Her gratification comes from bringing comfort or pleasure to her Master. If this seems strange to you, consider this—even in non-D/s relationships, couples have occasions where they are so caught up in their own pleasure they forget the needs of their partners. It is a normal human reaction. Within a D/s relationship, it is simply more obvious. The difference lies in the fact that the objectification is consensual."

He walked to the other side of the classroom and addressed Lea next. "A simple example would be a quickie or blow job. The Dom uses the sub to orgasm and then goes back to whatever he or she is doing. It can also be more complicated, such as playing the part of an inanimate object or even animal play."

Brie instantly thought of Captain and how much she'd enjoyed being his pet. It had been a lovely encounter she'd cherished.

Mr. Gallant continued, "To the casual observer it may appear one-sided, but the reality is that the exchange of power is arousing for both individuals. In giving up her power, the sub is able to fully embrace her Dom's pleasure and claim it for her own. For the Dominant, the gift of such an exchange serves to highlight the submissive's devotion to him, which is both appreciated and thoroughly enjoyed."

He walked back to his desk before he faced the girls. "Tonight you will be sharing in a practicum together. Please head upstairs to the limousine waiting for you.

This is an important assignment. We expect you not only to perform well, but to absorb and learn from the experience."

Brie was thrilled. Any practicum outside the Center's walls was exhilarating, but to do it with Lea and Mary would make it pure perfection!

The Dom hosting the party greeted the girls at the door. He was an older man with silver hair and a thin, serious face. "Thank you for coming," he said, shaking Brie's hand, then moving on to Lea's and Mary's. "I have several assistants who will instruct you as to your duties. My friends are used to flawless execution. See that you do not fail in the simple tasks given to you." With that, he gestured them inside and exited to another room, shutting the door behind him.

There were three women waiting with smiles on their faces. The short-haired blonde came up to Brie. "You have been given the noble task of serving food."

"Wonderful. What…?"

The girl put her finger to Brie's lips. "No more talking. Listen only. It will help you to succeed in your role."

Brie nodded. She looked up and saw that Lea and Mary were listening and *not* speaking. It was going to be an interesting evening, for sure.

"Please pay attention," the young woman admonished when she saw Brie wasn't focused on her. "First, we must get you undressed and thoroughly cleaned. It is going to take quite a while to get you ready for the event."

Brie had no idea what was being asked of her, but she became more excited as she was led through the luxurious apartment. Whoever this Dom was, he was a *very* successful man.

After Brie had peed, taken a soapy shower, and thoroughly dried off, the girl guided her into a large room with a panoramic view of the city. There was a small, oval table in the middle of the spacious room.

"Please lie down in the center of the table."

Brie lay down on it gracefully, finding it just large enough to hold her. The girl repositioned her and splayed out her hair in an artful pattern. As the woman worked, she gave Brie instructions. "You are to lie completely still. Do not react in any way to the people around you. Your sole purpose is to display the food elegantly. I highly recommend you keep your eyes glued to that spot on the ceiling." She pointed to a tiny speck directly above Brie.

"No matter what is said, how you are touched or if you itch…" She emphasized the last words, saying them slowly and succinctly. "Do…not…move."

I'm supposed to be a platter? Brie thought. *Well, here's to my first real experience with objectification.*

The blonde arranged small crackers and a variety of grapes over her body in an intricate and exacting pattern. Brie turned her head and saw that Mary was practicing balancing a flask of red liquid on her back while the assistant meticulously painted her arms and legs with delicate patterns. Apparently, she was playing the role of a table. Brie glanced over at Lea. She was stunning. Her naked body was painted gold and her large breasts looked amazing, all sparkly and alluring. A statue of a goddess, without a doubt, but Brie didn't envy Lea one bit. The assistant had positioned her arms at beautiful but awkward angles that would be hard to maintain for an entire evening.

Although Brie's role was lowly, at least it was easy. She watched in fascination as the blonde laid a small, round cloth over her bellybutton. Then she placed a ceramic ring around it and added a thin sheet of plastic. Brie squeaked when she poured a layer of ice cubes into it. A beautiful gold bowl was placed on top of that. The girl then spooned a decadent amount of caviar into the golden dish, filling it to the brim.

"I let you look at your friends, even though it means I have to fix your hair again. From this point forward, those eyes stay glued to the ceiling. Understand?"

Brie nodded and dutifully stared upwards as goose bumps prickled over her skin. The chill of the ice traveled straight to her groin. After the assistant had finished fixing her hair, she said, "You are nothing but a beautiful vessel. Understand that and enjoy the evening."

The three assistants quickly exited just before the doorbell rang.

It starts…

The Dom came out of what Brie assumed was his study and answered the door. A flow of guests quickly filled the apartment with their gentlemanly voices. Just hearing them sent Brie's body trembling, and she had to force herself to breathe slowly in the manner Tono had taught her. The men eventually made their way towards the girls and one last nervous sigh escaped Brie's lips before they entered the room.

The men treated the three naked girls as if they were a natural part of the decor. They talked business deals and discussed the upcoming national election. Brie heard their Dom offer the men drinks and knew that Mary was now the center of attention.

Brie listened intently to the conversations floating about. She couldn't resist. *A girl could learn a lot from these influential men…*

Just when she was getting used to being a part of the scenery, one of the men moved over to the table and lightly brushed his hand against her nipple as he picked up a cracker. He then spooned caviar onto it. She felt an electrical jolt and blinked several times in response. *Damn! This is going to be harder than I thought.*

As soon as he'd served himself, the table was surrounded by men who touched her casually as they partook of the expensive fish eggs. She desperately stared at the ceiling, reminding herself that she was an inanimate object that could not move, could not respond in any way to what was happening.

"Nice centerpiece, Sebastian," she heard.

Her Dom replied, "Yes, I agree. You'll never guess what it's called."

"Do tell."

"Brie."

There was a deep chuckle, and then Brie felt a hand rove over her thigh to her sweet spot. A finger penetrated her vagina and it took everything in her to remain completely still as the finger swirled around and then withdrew. She heard the distinct sound of sucking, and the guest said with a tone of amusement, "I think I will have to sample some of this Brie later."

"I'll make sure to set it aside for you."

Her loins contracted in pleasure at the statement. Brie did not understand why being treated in this way was such a turn-on, but there was no doubt the table she was lying on would show evidence of her arousal when she was finally allowed to move.

Brie heard comments from several of the men about the lovely statue. Someone must have touched Lea, because Brie heard her gasp softly.

"Am I mistaken, or did I hear something?" one of the gentlemen asked.

Their Dom replied nonchalantly, "Oh, didn't I tell you? I had this one installed with a voice box. Adds to the realism of the piece."

"I see… I can't say I agree," the man replied before moving off.

Brie felt bad for Lea. Failing in a practicum was never pleasant and she desperately wished she could share a joke to lighten Lea's spirit.

Brie had first thought she had been given the easiest assignment, but that simply was not the case. She struggled to stare at the ceiling while the light, incidental touches of the many men in attendance teased and aroused her.

Late into the evening, the apartment finally cleared out. "Why don't we move to the study for a smoke?" their Dom suggested to the last remaining guest.

"Why not?"

Brie recognized the voice and quivered. She was about to be tasted by the man who had sampled her.

Two of the assistants came into the room. Brie was cleaned off and then told to stand. With quick movements, the blonde deftly cleared the table and told Brie to lie back down.

Brie took a quick peek and saw poor Lea standing there, still in her statuesque form, completely ignored by the assistants. Mary had been cleaned off as well, but was still on all fours.

The helpers made themselves scarce when the door of the study opened. Brie hadn't been given any further instructions so she stared at the ceiling and waited.

"Ah, Sebastian, I see the Brie is ready for sampling."

"But of course."

Brie glanced briefly at her partner without being noticed. His sideburns, peppered with gray, contrasted charmingly with his black hair, giving him a distinguished look. He noticed her staring into his pale green eyes and did not smile when he told her, "I like vocal cheese."

It took her a second to realize he was making a joke. She looked back up at the ceiling and then squealed when he pulled her ass to the edge of the table and descended between her legs. He dragged his tongue against her sex, making her moan in delight.

But she whimpered when he pulled back the hood of her clit and sucked on her defenseless nub. He was relentless as he held her down and teased it. Just when she felt her pussy burn with orgasmic energy, he stopped.

Her senses came back to earth and she became aware of Mary and the host Dom going at it. Brie made a quick sideways glance. Mary was quite the loud, passionate table as he pounded her in the ass.

Her attention was instantly redirected when her partner grabbed her chin and forced her to look upwards. *Crap!* She was far too curious to make a good inanimate object.

She heard him unbuckle his pants and then unzip. He didn't even bother taking them off. He slid his cock inside her and began thrusting away. His strokes were long but unhurried. Brie kept her eyes on the speck, wondering why his detached taking of her made her so hot. She concentrated on his heavy breathing, grateful to be used in this way—his vessel of pleasure.

Her Dom leaned forward and cupped her face in his hands. "I haven't tasted all of you yet." He kissed her then, thrusting his tongue deep into her mouth. The man claimed her with his lips as he fucked her. It was intoxicating and her body steadily climbed towards its climax.

She felt him stiffen and then he groaned into her mouth as he came. Brie's body pulsed with need, but he pulled out and zipped back up. She was disheartened, but understood that as an object, personal fulfillment was not an option.

Brie noticed that Mary was no longer vocalizing, which indicated that her session was over as well. Then the host Dom asked her partner, "So, how was the Brie?"

Brie heard him get up from the floor as he answered in the positive. "Quite satisfying."

"Glad to hear it. So I'll be seeing you at the meeting tomorrow?"

"Yes. Until then." The two shook hands. After Brie's partner had left, their Dom addressed each of the girls.

"Miss Wilson, job well done. You may leave to clean up."

He walked over to his golden statue. "Ms. Taylor. Your performance was less than stellar." He caressed her large breasts and then tweaked one of her nipples. Lea didn't make a peep. He continued, "As far as I am concerned, you've learned your lesson and been properly punished. I see no reason to speak of it with your trainers."

Lea bowed her head and said softly, "Thank you, Master."

"My assistants will help you clean up." Two women instantly appeared and led her away.

He walked over to Brie last. "Miss Bennett, you performed satisfactorily. You may be excused as well. Go down the hall to your right, where you will find a private bathroom with your clothing."

Brie got up from the table, still a tangle of sexual nerves. He called after her, "You do not have permission to masturbate."

She turned around and bowed obediently. "Thank you, Master."

There was something oddly arousing at being denied her own pleasure. Tonight had opened up yet another sexual option to explore, and Brie was thrilled at the prospect of navigating it more thoroughly.

Marquis Plays with His Pet

The next day, Marquis presented Brie with another lesson on objectification in the auditorium. She had no idea what she was walking into when she joined him on the stage. Her breath caught in her throat when she saw the table he had set up for her. On it were four items: a crop; a leather, strappy contraption with a small metal bar; lubricant, and…a butt plug with a long, flowing tail. She knew exactly where he was taking her with this practicum, and it unnerved her.

"Tonight is about what I want, pearl."

"Yes, Master."

"And what I want is to attach this lovely bridle to your face, insert this plug deep in your ass and watch you swish that tail for me." He held up the crop and looked at her lustfully. "Then I will play with my pony using the crop before I fuck her hard."

Brie's heart beat a mile a minute. He was asking her to play out the scene she had ended with another Dom. Marquis always insisted on pushing her. Every one of his lessons took her further than she wanted to go. What surprised her was that a part of her wanted to be Marquis' pony.

"If it pleases you, Master."

"Undress where you are."

Brie immediately undid her corset and let it drop to the stage floor. She stepped out of it and removed her heels next, leaving her panties and hose for last. She stood there waiting silently for his next command, her short breaths coming in quick succession.

"Come to your Master and let him ready you for play."

She walked over to Marquis slowly, drawn to him like a magnet; frightened of the feelings he inspired yet hungry to let them play out.

"On your hands and knees."

She immediately dropped onto all fours, but her spirit balked at what he was going to do next. She closed her eyes, but he would not allow her that escape.

"Open your eyes, pearl, and watch your Master adorn you."

Brie turned her head and watched with trepidation as Marquis picked up the lube and coated the plug with it. He looked at her intently and he knelt down beside her. "How do you feel?"

Marquis was not asking her color, so she answered truthfully, "Frightened."

"That is not acceptable. You are not thinking like a sub. You are allowing your ego to get in the way of what you desire. What is it you desire, pearl?"

She looked into his dark eyes, knowing the answer without a doubt. "To please you."

"Yes. You know what I want and yet you are resistant."

"I'm sorry, Master."

"I do not need an apology. Tell me what you want."

She answered hesitantly, "I want you to adorn me, Master."

He shook his head. "That was *not* convincing."

Brie closed her eyes and focused on giving in to Marquis Gray's desire. *His pleasure is my pleasure…* She imagined his groans of passion and it made her wet to think of it. Taking this plug could either be enticing, or she could choose to make it something negative, which was not his intent. She opened her eyes and looked at him. "I want you to adorn your pony, Master."

He nodded and coated the outside of her anus with the lubricant before pressing the toy against her tight sphincter. Brie pushed back against it, seeking the invasion of the plug. She groaned as the tip slipped in.

"That's it," he coaxed. Marquis continued to press it in farther, sliding the plug in and out so that her muscles could loosen and allow for deeper penetration. She moaned when he made the final push and her ass muscles clamped around the end. "Swing that tail for me, pearl," he murmured in a low voice.

Brie wiggled her ass playfully and the long tail swished, brushing against her legs.

"Beautiful." He picked up the bridle next and ordered her to open her mouth. He placed the thin metal bit between her teeth and directed her to turn around so that he could buckle it on. The straps ran over her nose and under her chin, attaching at the back with a long rein that he let fall down in front. She began salivating and realized this was his version of the ball gag. *Why does the man have to be so thorough?*

Marquis picked up his crop and lightly smacked her on the ass. "Yes, this will do nicely." He picked up the reins from the floor and ordered her to crawl in a circle around him. He flicked the crop across her buttocks as she made her way around him. She wondered if the image reminded Lea and Mary of a horse in training.

"No, this won't do," he complained. "Stand up."

Brie got onto her feet, very aware of the plug in her ass and the metal bit in her mouth. Strangely, neither was causing her distress.

"Prance for me," he ordered. Brie automatically put her arms in front of her like a rearing horse and started gracefully prancing in a circle around him. She felt the gentle swish of the tail and wondered what it looked like in motion. He guided her with the reins as he smacked his crop against her ass with greater enthusiasm. "Faster, beauty."

Brie kept up with his demands for speed, responding to the sting of the crop that warmed her ass. Then he had her change direction and warmed the other side. By the time he asked her to stop, she was panting for breath.

He snapped his fingers and a short wooden table was brought onto the stage. "Onto the table, pearl. I wish to thoroughly examine my pony before I ride her."

Brie crawled onto the table and took on the stance of a proud mare, with her back arched and head held high—higher than a submissive was allowed. Marquis moved the reins to rest on her neck and put the crop down. His hands began to travel down her back and over her tender ass. "I appreciate the smooth round flank of a pony." He continued down over her thigh to her calf, finally stopping on her vulnerable feet. "The temperament of a beast can be determined by how they respond to having their hooves handled. Any resistance is considered a bad sign."

Brie understood the challenge and allowed him to lift her foot. Then he began tickling the arch. Her instinct was to pull away, but she endured his torture. He increased his cruelty by concentrating his efforts on her defenseless toes. Her loins contracted as she struggled not to move, but a giggle escaped past the metal bit.

He put her foot down and moved to the other side. Again his hands ran down her back, over the swell of her ass to her foot. The torture started up again. He found that spot in between her toes and brushed it ever so lightly. She jerked without meaning to.

He put her foot down slowly, without saying a word. *A bad sign.* He moved his hand up her back again, caressing the contours of her shoulder blades, then lower to appreciate the fullness of her breasts. Marquis Gray's fingers trailed down the length of her arm before he picked up her hand and lightly traced her palm with his finger. It tickled, but not with the intensity her toes had. No, this was sensual, intimate contact that made her moist between the legs.

Marquis moved over to the other side and he repeated the examination. Once satisfied with her 'hooves', he began an inspection of her genital region. Brie bit down on the metal as he commanded she open her legs wider. His fingers explored her swollen lips and vagina clinically. It wasn't the romantic touch of a lover. It was purposeful and without emotion, which turned her on even more.

He played with her juicy folds, commenting, "I see my filly is a wanton little thing."

Marquis ended his inspection by moving to her head. He opened her mouth and made as if he was checking her teeth. She could smell and taste herself on his fingers. When he seemed satisfied with the health of her mouth, he stroked her neck. Once again, his touch was back to being sensual and arousing. He pulled her hair from her face and examined her ears last, first tugging and pulling gently on them, before blowing his moist breath into each one. It sent a shiver, both times, all the way to her aching groin.

He stood back from her and shook his head slowly. "Almost perfect. Almost…"

She knew he was referring to her flinch and wondered what her punishment would be. "Stand up and face your Master."

Brie stood in front of Marquis Gray, her head no longer lifted in pride. He moved her long curls to her back and commanded her to put her hands to her sides. "That hoof reaction must be dealt with. As your equine trainer, it is my duty."

Brie nodded in pretended shame. She'd had no idea Marquis could be such a playful Dom. His many facets astounded her.

"Lift your head up and look to the ceiling, wanton

pony." She did, her breaths coming in quick gasps again. "Yes, I can see you know what must happen. Your heart races even now."

The leather tongue of the crop caressed her torso, the lightness of the contact making it alluring and welcomed. Several times he trailed the crop down to her mound, letting it rest there to tease her. But when he moved back up and flicked her hard nipple with it, she closed her eyes.

Yes, Brie knew very well what was about to happen…

He snapped the crop directly onto her right nipple and she moaned at the pleasurable sting it caused. Her pussy began pulsating—she wanted more of his wicked attention.

"A good filly should not resist her Master's touch. Do you understand?"

She nodded in breathless anticipation.

He snapped the crop against her left breast and she cried out, the tension in her pussy building up for release. "No coming," he commanded. She shuddered, trying to curb the erotic flow mounting inside her.

He snapped the crop against her breasts several more times before turning her around and commanding she bend over. She leaned against the table, needing him to enter her now. *But this isn't about me…*

Marquis Gray dragged the length of his crop across the crease of her ass. Her body responded favorably, remembering the cane, and she moaned. He began tapping her round buttocks with the crop, interspersing the motion with harder strokes. It teased her to distraction and she wiggled her ass suggestively, wanting him to take her.

His response was to give her two hard strokes that took her breath away, effectively putting her back in her place. He then went back to his tapping and stroking, reddening her pony ass with his crop. Just as with the cane, Marquis knew how to use his tool for maximum sexual arousal. Brie was gushing with need for her Dom.

He stopped unexpectedly and she felt him grab her sex, his middle finger slipping into her possessively. Brie's muscles pulsated around his finger—she was dangerously close to coming. She whimpered but did not pull away, even though the contact was sending her over the edge. Instead, she bit down on her own arm, distracting herself from the impending orgasm. It slowly abated and she heard him say, "Well done, wanton filly."

Marquis pulled her head back with the reins, making her pose attractively for the audience, and then continued to redden her ass with his crop. She loved the satisfying crack it made when it came into contact with her skin.

He laid his crop down and ran his hands over her buttocks. "It's so beautiful. I simply must taste." She felt his hot tongue caressing her stinging ass. Her need for him was so great it ate her up inside, and she whimpered loudly.

"Ponies don't whimper," he growled in her ear.

Brie had forgotten her place again. She was *his* instrument of pleasure. She must deny her need for release, not assume he would grant it. He slapped her throbbing cheeks. She was a selfish little sub and she knew it. But oh, how her body loved and craved the attention!

"On the floor, filly."

Brie got on all fours, aching for him. He pulled on the reins again, pulling her neck back in a graceful arch. "I am about to ride you, my wanton slut."

The normally offensive word sounded sexy coming from his lips, and she moaned in response. *I am your wanton slut… Mount me, Master!* she cried silently.

Marquis knelt behind her, still holding the reins tight. He swished her tail to one side and pushed his curved shaft inside her. Brie moaned in ecstasy and discomfort. The butt plug made her extremely tight but she enjoyed the feeling. It forced her to relax so she could take his deep thrusting—and she *needed* his thrusting.

"You're so tight, filly. Are you sure you can take all of me?"

Brie pushed against him, forcing his cock deeper.

"So be it." He let go of the reins and grabbed her ass with both hands, giving her the fullness of his cock without restraint. Brie's cries were somewhat muffled by the bit in her mouth, but they still rang loud and clear throughout the auditorium.

She felt him revving up for a quick climax and she had to quiet a whimper. His curved shaft was rubbing her G-spot deliciously because of the tightness. She started thrashing her head, trying to keep her orgasm at bay, but she was too close…

"Come," he demanded.

Tears of gratitude ran down her face, though she was unsure if his command had been out of kindness or simple coincidence. Regardless, she groaned against her bit, embracing the release she had tried heroically to hold back. He rammed his cock deep into her as her body squeezed his shaft with its rhythmic motion; she orgasmed so hard it almost hurt.

She trembled uncontrollably afterwards. With tender hands he unbuckled the bridle and removed the plug. He then picked her up in his arms. Marquis took her to the small room and lay with her once again. It was something she treasured about their encounters. He pulled her close and said, "I have not played with a pony before. Far more enjoyable than I imagined."

She smiled at the thought that she was his first. "You didn't miss a detail. From the bit to replace the ball gag to calling me a slut. But why?"

"Did you enjoy it?" he growled lustfully in her ear.

She blushed to admit it. "Yes, Master."

"You needed to overcome the hesitancy to obey such role play."

"Although it is not something you normally partake in?"

"Even trainers need to stretch themselves, pearl. No one should remain stagnant."

She turned towards him and looked into his perilous eyes. "I'd never imagined you had a frisky side, Master."

"We will not speak of it," he answered with a funny smile, crushing her to his chest.

What other surprises did Marquis Gray have hidden away?

Rituals and Tasks

Brie was on cloud nine, walking down the hallway with her heels making that lovely clicking sound against the tile as she made her way to Mr. Gallant's class. Out of nowhere, an unknown assailant drew her inside a dark room, placing a strong hand over her mouth. She struggled, screaming into the unyielding palm.

"Shh…" He lifted his hand away. "It's me."

She stopped struggling. His lips brushed against hers, lightly, teasingly. She leaned forward for more, but he pulled back, causing her to protest. "Wha…?"

Sir pushed her against the wall and returned his hand to her mouth. "No more words." She felt his other hand reach under her skirt and pull her thong down to her knees. Already her body was burning for him. Just his proximity made her crazy, but to be taken this way in the dark by her Sir…

His rigid cock pressed against her stomach as he leaned in, replacing his hand on her lips with his tongue. He plundered her mouth as his hand moved between her legs. She opened herself to his assault, needing to feel him.

"I can't deny myself any longer," he growled. He kissed her roughly as he pushed his finger deep inside her wet and willing body. She whimpered, her body a firestorm of lust. His thumb played with her clit as his finger simultaneously caressed her G-spot. Suddenly, he withdrew his hand and he hit the wall with his fist. "Damn you, Brie!"

She felt him move away and cried out, "Don't stop!"

Silence…

Her shallow gasps filled the room. Brie stayed pressed against the wall, willing him back to her.

She heard his ragged breath and knew he was just out of reach. Brie said nothing, waiting obediently, praying he would return to her.

"Fuck! You're like a drug to me."

She whispered into the dark, "Consume me."

He rushed upon her then. Sir found her wrists in the dark and pulled them above her head. He held onto them with one hand while the other fumbled with his zipper, then guided his shaft into her.

She cried out at the force of his entry. He covered her mouth to keep her quiet as he began thrusting hard, but it wasn't enough for either of them. He let go of her wrists and lifted her up by the thighs. He gained deeper access with the new angle and smashed her against the wall as he took her roughly.

Brie gasped as his cock claimed its prize. Then she heard Ms. Clark say, "Where the hell is Thane? He's not in his office."

Sir's hand was back on her mouth. His thrusts slowed but did not stop as the two listened to the conversation just outside the door.

Marquis Gray answered, "I have no idea. I'll head upstairs to ask at the front desk."

"I'll check the commons again," Ms. Clark snapped. "This is such a waste of time! He's going to get an earful when I see him."

Brie heard Sir chuckle softly, just before he thrust deep. He kissed her again, his lips expressing a tenderness she hadn't experienced before. When he pulled away, she breathed out in the barest of whispers, "I love you, Sir."

He responded by grabbing her face in his hands and kissing her deeply as his body crushed her against the wall. His tongue thrust into her mouth with the same passion as his cock drove into her burning depths. She lost herself in his desire as he consumed her—mind, body and soul.

"I need more…" he grunted.

She was desperate to give him more, wrapping her arms around his neck. "Just say the word and I am yours completely."

His lips moved to her ear. She heard his intake of breath just as he was about to speak. Brie closed her eyes, waiting to hear his declaration of love.

The door swung open and light flooded the room. "Brie,

what are you doing in the dark?" Mr. Reynolds asked.

Brie rubbed her eyes, waking from her dream. She looked up at her boss as the blood rushed to her cheeks. "I just needed to rest my eyes for a few minutes. Did I go past my break?" She started to get up, but he told her to sit back down.

"You're fine. You still have a few minutes left."

Brie took several deep breaths to calm her racing heart. Even in her dreams she had been denied hearing Sir say those three little words. She felt her heart catch. *Is it a sign that I never will?*

Mr. Reynolds sat down next to her in the tiny office. "Is there anything I can do? You know I will be happy to help if I can."

She smiled at the compassionate man who was so much like a father to her. "It's nothing to worry about, Mr. Reynolds. Classes are just taking a lot out of me. It'll be over soon."

He responded sadly, "I have an uneasy feeling that I won't be seeing your smiling face around here much longer." He patted her hand. "But that's okay. You were meant for more than this. It's just that this old man will miss you."

"Who says I'm leaving?" she quipped. "You can't run this place with Jeff as your sidekick."

He looked at her kindly. "Brie, you deserve better than this."

Tears welled up when she heard the earnestness in his voice. "Thank you, Mr. Reynolds."

He gave her hand one final pat. "So have you got enough Zs or should I turn the light back off and give you five more minutes?"

"I think I'm good."

"Glad to hear it. Jeff screwed up stocking yesterday. Do you mind taking care of that?"

"I don't know how you put up with that boy," Brie grumbled good-naturedly as she got up from her chair.

"What choice do I have when he's related to the owner? I consider Jeff a cross I must bear. The boy teaches me patience on a level no one else could." He stood up and grinned. "Besides, who else would put up with him?"

"You're a good man, Mr. Reynolds," she said, and gave him a peck on his weathered cheek.

As she left work that night, Brie felt a cool chill travel down her spine. Her boss was right; she felt it in her bones that her days at the tobacco shop were numbered. She struggled with the conflicting emotions of excitement and sadness, knowing things were about to change.

She walked up to the doors of the Training Center with a playful grin on her face. Blue Eyes had been the one to mess with her mind for weeks now. It was high time to give him a taste of his own medicine. As she passed, she tucked her hair behind her ear while batting her eyes at him.

He cleared his throat before saying his customary, "Good evening, Miss Bennett."

She turned around in one fluid motion, blowing him a kiss before turning back around and walking to the elevator. *Take that, Wolfpup,* she thought, giggling to herself.

Mr. Gallant's class centered on the importance of

tasks and rituals. "Daily tasks given by the Dominant are gifts. They may look like common, everyday tasks to an outsider, but for the submissive it is the opportunity to serve her Master. It allows her to please her Dom and gives her an opportunity to be rewarded for a job well done."

"Rituals, on the other hand, are formalized series of words or actions that reinforce the D/s dynamic. They are created to set the mood and build anticipation. They should be simple and meaningful to both parties."

"Miss Bennett, can you give me an example of a task versus a ritual?"

Luckily, Brie had been paying close attention. "An example of a task would be laying out your Dom's clothes for the following day, meeting his exact specifications. A ritual could be greeting your Dominant at the door every day in a submissive pose until he touches your head and commands you to serve him."

"Very good."

Mr. Gallant opened his desk drawer and pulled out three cell phones. He placed one on each of their desks. "Tonight you will be doing a set of tasks for one of your trainers. You are expected to obey to the letter—no excuses. That may mean being creative in order to fulfill the commands given to you."

Brie didn't understand why a phone would be needed, but she felt the thrill that always came with a new challenge.

"You will meet the trainers at the commons. Remember that the goal is to follow the task to the letter. Failure is not an option." The three girls got up to leave and he added, "Go ahead and take your coats with you. You will be leaving the Center shortly."

Lea squealed after they left his classroom. "Another field trip!"

Brie couldn't hide her excitement. "I wonder what we'll be asked to do this time. I love outdoor practicums!"

Mary scoffed, "It sounds dumb to me."

Brie frowned. "Why do you have to put everything down? You never give anything a chance, even though you end up enjoying it."

"Hey, don't knock how I approach life. If I expect the worst, when it happens I'm not disappointed."

Brie shook her head. "That sounds like a depressing way to live."

Mary snorted. "It works for me. If things go well then it's an unexpected surprise, and I'm happy about it."

Brie stopped in the middle of the hallway. "What if, by expecting things to go badly, you guarantee they do?"

Lea piped in, "Yeah, like what if you're creating your own reality with your negative thinking?"

Mary rolled her eyes. "If that were true, I would never experience anything good. The fact that I do shoots your little theory to hell. Why do you two even care, anyway?"

"Because your negative attitude affects us," Lea answered.

Mary growled angrily, "And *this* is why I hate women! I don't want to hold hands and skip around pretending everything is wonderful. It's dumb."

"No, you're dumb!" Lea snapped.

Her venomous outburst surprised Brie. They couldn't afford to fight—not now. This was their last week together.

Maybe that's why Mary is acting hostile. What if Mary didn't want their time together to end any more than she did?

Brie stopped again and turned on them both. "Enough! We are here to support each other. Tonight, we are going to kick butt on our tasks. Our trainers will talk about our awesomeness for years, do you understand me?"

Lea smiled at her. "Uh-huh! Kicking ass and taking names…"

"You two are so juvenile," Mary said contemptuously as she walked ahead of the two. Then she looked back and added with a wink, "Of course, I'm going to kick better butt than either of you. It'll be *my* name the trainers will be talking about for years."

Brie pulled the belt from her coat discreetly, folding it in half. When Mary wasn't looking, she whipped her ass with it. "You wish! It's Brie all the way, woman."

Mary jumped away in surprise and then faced her with a grin. "Stinky cheese? I think not." She scooted to the side when Brie tried to hit her again.

Lea giggled adorably. "Yes, you will be remembered as Mary Quite Contrary and Stinky Brie, but it will be Lea the Lovely that will stand above the rest."

"Bend over, Lea. I must beat you for that," Brie commanded.

They heard a door open and Faelan popped his head out of the classroom. His voice was unusually stern.

"You *are* aware that we can hear every word you say."

Brie instantly apologized, bowing her head in mortification. How embarrassing to have had Blue Eyes, along with the other training Dominants, hear their feminine exchange.

He replied, "As penance, you three must go home tonight and strap on a vibrator at full blast for a half-hour without coming." He disappeared back into the classroom.

As the three hurried to the commons, Lea whispered, "Do you think he was serious?"

Brie shrugged. "I'm not sure."

Sir greeted the girls with a nod of his head. If he had heard their ruckus, he didn't mention it. However, Brie felt certain he would hear of it later.

He said pleasantly, "Mr. Gallant spoke to you about rituals. Tonight I will assign each of you a ritual I expect you to follow at the beginning of each session for the remainder of your training."

He addressed Mary first. "As soon as you enter the room, you are to move to the side and bow low with your arms outstretched on the floor. You are not allowed to speak or move until one of the trainers acknowledges you. Do so now."

He moved on to Lea next. "When you enter the classroom, you are to strip off your panties and leave them by the door. You are then to present yourself in a kneeling position with your knees shoulder length apart. You may not release from the position until you have been given permission. Do so now."

Brie held her breath as she waited for Sir to command her. Anytime she was given his full attention, she felt unadulterated bliss. She dared to look him in the eye, melting in the heat of his gaze. "Miss Bennett, when you enter the room you are to take off your corset and leave it at the entrance. Kneel in front of the panel with your legs closed, put your arms behind your back so that your breasts are fully presented. You are not to move until you are given permission. Do so now."

Brie quickly untied the corset and placed it by the frame of the door. Then she gracefully glided over to the panel. She knelt down slowly, basking in the joy of her femininity. She would bet that even Ms. Clark was enjoying the view…but knowing her, probably not as much as the sight of Lea's hot little beaver.

Sir continued with his instructions, telling the girls which Dom they had been paired up with for the evening. "Miss Bennett, you will be working with Master Coen tonight." Her bottom tingled in remembrance of the trainer's spanking. What would the muscular Coen have for her tonight?

After he had assigned each girl her Dom, Marquis Gray stood up and walked over to Lea. He placed his hand on her head and said, "You may stand and serve me."

Master Anderson approached Mary and said, "On your feet, slave. Attend to your Master."

Brie felt Master Coen beside her. He grabbed her long hair and pulled her chin up with gentle force. "It's time." She rose from the floor, gathered her corset, and followed him to a secluded corner to listen to his orders.

"You will get into your car and check your text.

There you will find my next set of instructions. Be aware that when you hit the record button, the images will go directly to my phone. You also cannot text when it is recording."

Brie looked at her cell phone and saw a large, red record button on the upper right. This was *not* an ordinary cell phone.

"Everything you need to know will be explained in the text." His eyes held a mischievous glint when he ordered her to leave.

Brie glanced over and saw that the other girls were being given explicit instructions. It didn't seem fair, but she was desperate not to fail her practicum so she obeyed her Master and left the Center. Once inside her car, she flipped the phone open and read his first text.

Proceed to the Supermart ten minutes from the school. Purchase hairbrush (thick handle), clothespins, Velcro w/ adhesive on back, condoms and a red bandana. Once items are attained, text your Master.

Brie felt nervous excitement as she put the phone down and started her car. Master Coen was a wildcard. She wasn't sure if he liked her or not, but she would do everything in her power to please him.

She drove to the huge store and got out of her car, tightening the belt of her coat. She hadn't gone anywhere public in her school uniform before, and was taken aback when a man walking towards her gave her a complete up and down before whistling. Brie looked to the ground and tried to calm the blush threatening to take over. Wearing her uniform in the vanilla world made her feel exposed, even with the long coat.

She made her way into the store and quickly collected the things on the list. She stood in line and watched her items go into the bag, one by one. Her excitement was heightened at knowing that they were most likely going to be used on her.

She thanked the cashier before texting her trainer. *Items purchased, Master.*

Immediately the phone vibrated with her next task: *Find secluded area in store. You will be playing w/ yourself for my pleasure. Set up phone to record and then text. You have 10 min.*

Brie's breath caught in her throat. Ten minutes to find a place and set up the camera? It seemed impossible! She looked around wildly, trying to figure out where she could do it. She knew there would be a break room and a stockroom, but she might get caught by an employee, which would cause all kinds of unwanted trouble. The only place she could think to do it was the bathroom, but how could she pleasure herself on a toilet? It wouldn't do.

Time was ticking and Brie started to sweat. She suddenly had a flash of brilliance and literally ran to the kitchen department. She grabbed a large cutting board and then headed to the bedroom department, where she snatched up a small pillow. With both items procured, she made her way through the express lane. The cashier looked through her other bags, double-checking she hadn't stolen anything. Brie tried to remain calm, but knew she was losing precious minutes.

When she got the okay, she took her many bags and ran to the bathroom. She sought out the large handicapped stall and slammed the door shut. She laid her cutting board over the seat of the toilet, put the pillow against the back of it, and then lined up each of the items on the edge of the board for easy access. Next she peeled off the backing of the adhesive and placed a piece of Velcro on the phone. She quickly checked for the right camera angle, estimating where to stick it on the metal door. She looked at the phone and saw she still had a minute left.

Brie ran to the sinks and quickly washed her hands. A woman came in and headed towards her stall.

Brie cried out, "No, no, no!" She rushed past and slammed the door of the stall behind her. She immediately texted Master Coen: *Master, camera is set up. Will do quick record & check back to see if you like angle.*

She hit the record button and pressed the phone against the Velcro. Then she gingerly sat down on the cutting board, careful not to move her items, and waved at the phone. She got up, stopped recording and texted, *To your liking?*

He responded, *Camera is fine. Attach clothespins to nipples. Place condom over hairbrush handle. Tie bandana over eyes. Count to 200 while you play w/ clit then fuck yourself with hairbrush. Scream my name when you come. If you please me, I will use hairbrush when you return.*

Brie's heart was pounding as she placed the camera back on the door and hit the record button. She could hear the woman washing her hands and prayed no one else would come in until she had finished. As much as she dreaded the thought of being caught, there was a thrill at doing something so private in a public setting.

She laid her coat on top of the bags before untying her corset and pulling off her panties. She left everything else on in case she needed to make a quick exit. She sat back down on her board and leaned against the pillow while looking at the phone with a playful smile. *Master Coen has such a wicked mind!*

Brie picked up the first clothespin and attached it to her innocent nipple. She squealed when the wooden tip closed down on it. *OMG, that hurts!* She took several deep breaths before she attached the other one. Brie bit her lip and groaned. She slowed her breathing down and accepted the throbbing pain.

She opened her eyes and unwrapped a condom, then slowly covered the handle of the hairbrush, imagining that it was Master Coen's cock. When it was completely covered, she looked at the camera and nodded. Then she placed it down and picked up the bandana. Brie rolled the cloth up and tied it over her eyes. Losing her sight made everything more intense and had the added benefit of calming her.

She spread her legs apart and began playing with her clit, mouthing the numbers slowly to two hundred. First, she twirled her fingers lightly over her pussy, wetting her fingers with her excitement. Then she slowly inserted a finger, moaning softly as she did. After several thrusts, she flicked her clit again. This time she got into it, feeling the heat begin. Desperate for penetration, she thrust two fingers back inside, pumping herself the way a man would drive his cock into her. However, the stimulation to her clit had had more effect, so she pulled out and began rubbing it vigorously, mewing under her breath.

Brie imagined how she looked—wearing a blindfold with her legs spread and her nipples clamped—while eagerly playing with herself. It was so naughty that she could almost have come just by thinking about it. *...one hundred ninety-eight, one hundred ninety-nine, two hundred...*

She fumbled around for the hairbrush and then slowly inserted it into her willing depths. She braced her legs against the sides of the stall so Master Coen could get a better view. She started out slow and sensual, biting her lip and moaning as she pushed the hairbrush farther inside. Then she let herself really have it, thrusting quickly, concentrating her motions around her opening, where all the nerve endings were firing electrical pulses. Her left foot slipped and she squeaked as she righted herself. She started up again, pushing harder against the walls with her legs so she wouldn't be interrupted a second time. With one hand, she thrust the pseudo-phallus while she stimulated her clit with the other, all the while imagining Master Coen's veiny cock taking her deeply as he ordered her to come.

Her legs started shaking and she whimpered audibly. *So close, so close...*

Brie heard the high-pitched voices of young women just outside the door. It was now or never. She mercilessly flicked her clit, pushing the brush deep inside. Her inner muscles clenched around it as the orgasm washed over her. "Master Coen!" she screamed.

She heard the door open, followed by giggling laughter. Brie ripped off her blindfold and plucked off the clothespins. Then she quickly gathered her materials and stuffed them in the shopping bags. She didn't want to waste time putting on the corset, so she stuffed it in the bag as well. She threw on her coat, buttoned it up and then approached the camera, mouthing the words, "Thank you, Master," before turning the record button off.

She was surprised when the phone immediately rumbled in her hand. *Come back to the Center so you may be rewarded.*

Brie hugged the phone to her chest before slipping it into her coat pocket. She could hear the girls chatting away by the sinks. Obviously, they wanted to see who had made such a fool of herself in a bathroom stall.

She realized she could choose to be embarrassed or not. Brie had just completed her first task for Master Coen and he had been pleased. That was enough for her. She smoothed out her hair and pinched her cheeks to give them a little more color.

Brie opened the door and looked at the girls with a half-smile. She said nothing as she set her bags down and washed her hands. She was slow and deliberate, consciously graceful with every move. She looked at the group of four women and smiled before she picked up her bags. She heard no laughter when she left, only silence. Brie beamed inside. *And that is how it's done.*

In the car, she checked her messages and saw that he had left another text for her. *Join me in the auditorium.*

Brie hurried back to the school and found Master Coen on the stage, waiting for her. She noticed that only Ms. Clark and Sir were in attendance. She figured that

Lea and Mary must still be out completing the practicums with their trainers.

She marched onto the stage, but turned when Sir called her name. "Miss Bennett, how would you rate your experience?"

Her eyes widened in excitement when she answered. "An eight! I loved the challenge and the overall thrill of it."

Master Coen replied, "Your use of additional props heightened my enjoyment of the scene."

She turned to him and bowed. "Thank you, Master Coen. It was my pleasure."

"But a pillow?" Ms. Clark complained. "You looked like the Queen of Sheba reclining in luxury when discomfort was supposed to be part of the experience."

Brie was quick to answer, keeping her eyes glued to the stage floor. "Master Coen did not command my discomfort. I assumed it was allowed."

Ms. Clark said in a sarcastic voice, "You know what they say about assuming, Miss Bennett."

Sir spoke in Brie's defense. "The student is correct. There was no command that stipulated otherwise. She showed creativity and quick thinking. It was a pleasant scene to watch."

Brie had had no idea that the other trainers would be observing her performance as well, but it made sense.

"What happened with the young ladies who entered the restroom near the end?" her beefy Dom asked.

"Nothing, Master Coen. They said nothing when I left."

"Yeah, I bet they laughed your ass right out of

there," Ms. Clark replied with a snort.

"Actually no, Mistress." Brie threw in the title to stroke her ego. "They were quite respectful."

Brie glanced up and saw the slightest smile play across Sir's lips. It thrilled her heart to amuse him. "While Ms. Clark and I observe the last two students, you may enjoy your reward with Master Coen." With that, Sir pulled out a portable screen and he and Ms. Clark proceeded to watch it together.

A stool was brought onto the stage and Master Coen commanded that she strip completely and then lean against it. He fished the hairbrush from the bag and smiled at her. "I promised to use it on you for a job well done. Bend over so I may administer your reward."

Brie leaned her torso fully against the stool, exposing her defenseless ass to him. A hairbrush sounded more cruel than fun. She closed her eyes, waiting for the first hit. Instead, he slid the handle between her legs and caressed her with it.

"Oh, yes, I liked the way you placed the condom on the instrument and then nodded at me. How you counted slowly so I could enjoy the way you played with yourself. But the technique you used to fuck yourself with the hairbrush…now, *that* was a real education." He paused and rolled a condom over it before he slipped it into her. "So you like it shallow and fast, do you?"

"Yes, Master."

She looked behind her and watched his muscular arm as he thrust the pseudo-phallus at a pace she had been unable to reach. She groaned in pleasure and opened her legs wider for him. Master Coen kept up the rhythm and depth for several minutes. All those muscles definitely made him the man for the job. Then he suddenly threw the brush across the stage and commanded Brie to sit on the stool with her legs spread open.

He unzipped his pants and pulled out his sizeable shaft. "I'm going to fuck you in the same fashion, Miss Bennett." He guided his cock between her swollen lips and pushed it farther into her—but just the tip.

Master Coen held her waist with his massive hands as he fucked her with just the head of his cock. He was a machine in his taking of her, his pounding shallow but with decided force. She threw her head back and cried out his name when he eventually gave her permission to come.

Before the last contraction ended, he thrust his manhood deep inside her and said in a hushed voice, "I find you worthy," as his shaft shuddered in its own release.

"Thank you," Brie gasped out between breaths. *Finally, vindication!*

While the two panted on the stage, Brie snuck a peek at Sir. His eyes were on her, but devoid of any emotion.

She got off the chair and slowly dressed. Brie wondered if her need to please whichever Dom she was with had served to drive a wedge between them. The thought undid her until she remembered their talk on the first night of her training. Sir had complimented her ability to please every Dom she had trained with and claimed he wanted to test the limits of what she would do. How could Sir hold that against her now?

Tono's Lesson on Flying

Late that night, she stared at her little bullet, contemplating whether she really needed to follow through with Faelan's punishment. He was just a Dom-in-training, after all. However, Sir had commanded that they treat the student Doms with the same respect they afforded other Dominants.

"Damn you, Blue Eyes…" Brie growled as she lay on her bed. She placed the tiny bullet against her clit and closed her legs. It simply wasn't worth getting in trouble with the trainers.

She turned on the device and sighed. This was a stupid punishment. *What a newbie!* Brie looked over at her bedside clock and noted the time. She was supposed to endure it for thirty minutes.

Brie turned her toy on full blast and squeezed her eyes shut. *Oh, damn, maybe this is going to be more difficult than I thought.* Her clit was already vibrating with the hint of an orgasm. But what had she expected? A night at the Training Center could do that to a girl.

She sighed in frustration and thought of Faelan;

mainly how mad she was at him. However, thinking about those blue eyes had the opposite effect than what she had been going for and she felt her pussy start contracting in a quick orgasm. She turned off the bullet and stared at the ceiling. *Damn…* Now she would have to start over again.

Once her body had calmed down, she turned it back on and then immediately back off. *Too soon!* Brie got up and took a freezing cold shower. With her skin blue and her teeth chattering, she lay back down and placed the tiny bullet between her legs, back on full blast. She kept her eyes shut and endured. After an excruciating amount of time, she checked the clock. *Six freakin' minutes. Holy crap!*

"I hate you!" she screamed at the ceiling. She could just imagine Todd's smug grin at knowing that three girls were enduring his punishment tonight. Brie concentrated on Jeff, the pathetic example of manhood at the tobacco shop. There was nothing sexy about the lazy shit and it helped to quell any stirrings in her loins. She glanced over and saw that she had made it another fifteen minutes. *Ten more to go.*

Brie focused on Jeff's face and was horrified when his eyes morphed into crystal blue orbs. Jeff smiled at her, but it was *his* smile. Brie heard Faelan's voice whispering in her ear, while he teased her nipples with the feather.

She whimpered and looked at the clock. *Four more minutes…*

For a newbie, he'd sure had an uncanny knack for teasing her. It surprised Brie that spending a night trying not to think of Faelan meant she was *only* thinking of him.

She stared at the clock and counted out the last two minutes. It was the only way to survive the ordeal. As soon as the second hand hit the twelve, she unclenched her legs and threw the bullet down on the other side of the bed. "A-ha! Take that!"

Seeing Blue Eyes the next evening was not easy. It was difficult to look him in the eye, but she didn't want Todd to have that kind of power over her. Unfortunately, her mind went to mush when she gazed into eyes like blue oceans. There was definitely a different vibe to the man now. Neither of them said anything as he opened the door and let her pass.

As much as Brie had struggled with Faelan's punishment, she was eternally grateful she had followed through with it, because it was the first thing Mr. Gallant asked the class about. "Raise your hand if you did your penance for last night's interruption in the hallway."

Brie looked over and saw the other two girls hesitantly raise their hands, too. She was surprised that Faelan had that kind of authority over their little group.

"Good. I do not want to hear about that kind of behavior again. Such foolishness not only reflects badly on you, but you also disrupted several classes that were in session."

All three girls bowed their heads in shame. Really, it had been Brie's fault, so she spoke up. "Mr. Gallant?"

"Yes, Miss Bennett?"

"It was m—"

"I don't care to hear another word about it." He

started class as if nothing had happened. Brie looked over at her friends and shrugged.

At the end of the session, Mr. Gallant directed Brie to head straight to the auditorium instead of following Lea and Mary to their normal room. Brie was worried she was going to be made an example of by the panel.

"Do you know why, Mr. Gallant?" she asked.

"Yours is not to question but to obey, Miss Bennett."

She nodded and left the classroom with her stomach in knots.

Brie listened to the lonely echo of her heels as she made her way down the empty hall. She opened the auditorium door and peeked inside. The sound of flute music filled the space. She literally squealed with happiness when she saw who was standing onstage.

"Tono!"

He put his finger to his lips and gestured for her to come to him. She clamped her mouth shut and ran down the aisle, then jumped into his arms. His embrace was magical, both safe and magnetic.

When his lips came down on hers, she willingly lost herself in his kiss. He pulled away too soon for her, but then cradled her cheek gently. "Toriko." She looked into his chocolate eyes, adrift in their connection. The two stood in silence for several moments, having no need to speak.

Finally, he broke the spell. "You will miss the first practicum tonight because Kinbaku takes time, as you know, little slave."

She could not contain her joy. Getting another

chance to experience Tono's mastery was more than she had hoped for. Brie looked down at the stage floor and saw that he had brought the green straw mat from his home. There was also a large brass ring and coils of jute—the smell of which was already calling to her.

"We do not have time for tea, I am afraid," he said, with an impish smile. She pressed her head against his chest and grinned. Tono's heartbeat was slow, strong, and reassuring.

"Come join me on the mat, toriko."

She knelt down and closed her eyes when she felt his arms wrap around her from behind. She listened to his breathing and slowed her breath to match his. The mutual connection was immediate.

"Yes, toriko," he said soothingly.

She tilted her head far back and kissed his chin. "I have missed you."

He chuckled softly and picked up the jute, then placed it in her hands. "Kiss your restraint."

She lovingly kissed the rope that would hold her in her own private heaven. She then pressed it against her cheek and whispered a word of thanks before handing it back to him.

"Tonight will be different. Tonight you shall fly, little one."

"Tono?"

"You will be suspended by the jute."

Brie gasped, a feeling of destiny flowing through her. She leaned her head against his chest. "I've secretly dreamed about it, Tono."

"Good, because I have yearned to share this with

you. Unfortunately, I must rush the process because your trainers want to share the Kinbaku experience with others."

"I don't mind."

"Toriko," he said, brushing his lips against her ear, "tonight you will only wear one item." He opened his hand and she saw the red thong he had taken from her the first night they'd met.

"It will be my honor, Tono." Brie stood up and undressed for him, sliding the thong into place under the watchful eyes of her handsome Dom. His eyes sparkled in appreciation.

When she moved back over to him, he grabbed her waist and kissed her stomach. "Tonight, when you feel moments of distress, what must you do?"

"Breathe with you."

"Correct. Sit down on the mat and spread out the fingers of your right hand so we can begin."

Brie closed her eyes as he wove the jute between her fingers and began the slow and delicious act of binding her. The tug and pull as he worked his magic played on her senses, taking her down the road of inner nirvana. Her body remembered and followed its path without hesitation.

He bound her right hand in a pose that lightly caressed her cheek. She wondered at the purpose, but remained silent as he began binding her chest with his slow, deliberate movements. The chest binding was her favorite part. Giving up the ability to take a deep breath demanded such an intense level of submission. She moaned softly.

"Yes, toriko."

He bound her tighter than he had before. She listened to his slow, even breaths to calm the fear that threatened to burst forth. She wanted this—needed it, in fact.

She glanced down and saw her breasts framed by the jute, but then he placed a single rope across her nipples and tightened it. It was strangely erotic to have her nipples held by the unforgiving jute. When she looked up, he kissed her and she felt her body burn with powerful need. "I wa—"

He put his finger over her lips without speaking and continued his art. Tono bound her left arm in a pleasing position behind her back. Then he gently pushed her down on the mat and started on her legs.

She looked up at the dark void of the auditorium ceiling. Brie closed her eyes again and concentrated on the gentle music as her legs were claimed by the jute. Bound, unable to move, breath restricted, completely his…

"I will demonstrate the art of rope suspension."

Brie opened her eyes and was surprised to see the auditorium full of trainers and students from both the submissive and Dominant classes. She hadn't been aware of their arrival.

Tono continued speaking in his soothing voice as his hands ran over her body. "As with most activities, experience is essential. Nerve damage can result with suspension, so do not attempt without proper instruction." Brie noticed that Tono had attached the large brass ring to chains above her. Through it, he had threaded the various strands of jute that bound her body.

"Kinbaku is an exacting method, but when done correctly the process will bind your submissive without pain."

Tono addressed Brie. "Color, toriko?"

"Green." She added in a whisper, "A lovely jute green."

He smiled and then turned back to the audience. "Never leave your submissive alone once you have begun the binding process. You must also have EMT scissors ready, should you need to release them quickly."

He gestured to the different points at which he had bound her. "The key is balance. To prevent damage, you must support the body."

Tono looked down at Brie. "Are you ready to fly, toriko?"

She nodded, holding her breath as he took the ropes and began pulling her off the ground. The constriction increased as gravity took over. It felt as if the world suddenly dropped away from her, and she whimpered, "Tono…"

"Breathe," he reminded her. He pressed his body against her so she could harmonize with him again. She closed her eyes and shut out the rest of the world as she reconnected with Tono. She felt him pull away and lift her higher, then the tugging and pulling began as he secured the ropes.

Brie kept her breaths slow and shallow as her body began floating within itself. She heard the sound of people clapping and realized that the pose he had created must look impressive.

"With your submissive bound like this, you are free to explore her sensuality without limitation." He did something then that both surprised and pleased her. Tono grabbed onto the large brass ring and, using only his arm strength, pulled himself on top of her, his body lying lengthwise. The two were together in midair. His arm shook from the effort of supporting himself, but he smiled down at her. "And now I join you in your flight, toriko." He leaned over and kissed her for a brief moment before lowering himself back down. It was so powerfully sexy; she wished he would do it again.

Instead, she felt him move between her legs and lift her wet thong out of the way. She moaned when his tongue made contact with her. She had thirsted for the gift of his mouth ever since their last time together. The moment he began lightly sucking on her clit, her body discharged the surge of orgasmic energy that had built up since their last meeting.

Brie mewed as her body tensed and relaxed in joyous release. She'd never come so fast before, but it did not dissipate like a normal climax. Instead, his constant suction demanded she fall deeper into the ocean of sensuality he had created. She willingly relaxed and let the ice-cold wave take her back to the place where desire meets otherworldliness.

His voice sounded distant, as if in a dream. "Come back to me."

"Join me…" she whispered.

"Come back," he repeated firmly.

She became aware of his hands trailing over her body. When she opened her eyelids, she was greeted by his smiling brown eyes looking down at her. He'd already set her back on the ground and was now undoing the larger bindings. Once she was free of them, he picked her up and carried her to the private room.

Instead of laying her on the bed, he sat on the floor with her and untied the rest of the jute. The feel of his hands was relaxing, slowly bringing her back into full awareness, although it was difficult to lose the rigidity of the jute—each release of rope felt like a loss of their connection.

"I didn't want it to stop, Tono."

He laughed softly. "You embraced it much faster and more fully this time, little slave." When he pulled the last of the rope away, he traced the lines it had left on her skin. "I think the trails left behind are just as beautiful as the jute itself."

She caressed his masculine jaw with her fingertips. "I love this."

His gaze fell on her. "Kinbaku, or us?"

She opened her mouth to answer, but he stopped her. "Don't answer. I should not have asked."

He stood up, gathered the jute in one hand and held out his other to help her up. It was with great reluctance that she took his hand and left the tiny room. When she went to sit back down, she noticed a photo on her seat.

"What's this?" she whispered to Lea.

"Tono said it was his inspiration for today's demonstration."

Brie looked at it closely and saw that it was a photo of her. The first one he had taken, in fact. Her hand was against her cheek as she looked at the camera with dreamy lust in her eyes. Looking at the photo instantly took her back to that day, to that specific moment in time with him.

This could be her life if she chose it...

Auction Day:
The Wolf Shows His Teeth

Brie pampered herself the morning before the auction. A long bubble bath with classical music made for a relaxed little submissive. She met Lea and Mary at the school and couldn't help noticing the Center was buzzing with excitement.

"What's going on?" she asked Mary.

"I don't know. It's weird. Even Ms. Clark is smiling."

"An actual smile?"

Mary nodded slowly as if she couldn't believe it, either.

Lea poked Brie in the ribs and pointed out that Sir and Marquis were having a private conversation and were actually laughing together. It was surreal.

When Ms. Clark came to get them, Brie saw her lips turned up in a jovial manner, even when she looked at Brie. *Twilight Zone moment, for sure…* Brie soon found herself on the stage, anxiously waiting to find out what the excitement was all about. She became distraught when she got the answer.

"This will be the last auction for this class of submissives. In honor of that, we will begin the bidding at one thousand dollars," the auctioneer announced.

The last auction? She knew the class would be ending next week, but she'd assumed there would be a final auction. She hadn't been prepared for things to end this fast!

There was a flurry of bidding and the numbers kept rising until she heard the auctioneer call out, "Sold to Faelan for two thousand, four hundred dollars."

Her first thought was, *Oh crap, that's a lot of money!* Her second was utter disbelief. *Faelan?*

He confidently walked onto the stage and took Brie's arm. Her heart skipped a beat at his handling of her. The aura surrounding Blue Eyes was intensely male.

Brie followed him down the steps while the bidding began for Mary. The girl ended up in the hands of Captain. This time, he did not bother with the blindfold. She could not see the expression on Mary's face when he went to retrieve her, but Brie sincerely hoped Mary would be kind to the man.

"Are you ready, blossom?"

Brie looked up into Faelan's blue eyes and caught her breath. The intensity of his stare made him seem dangerous. She followed meekly behind him, her body quivering with excitement—and a little fear. There was definitely a dangerous vibe to him.

It turned out that Faelan drove an old Mustang convertible. He raised his eyebrow in a sexy manner when he opened the door, explaining to her, "Sucker for classics."

When she'd sat down, he leaned over and buckled her into the seat, his lips just centimeters from hers. She could almost feel them on her mouth, but he pulled away and said, "Sucker for safety, too."

Faelan wasn't a speed demon like Tono, but he did punch it on the straightaways. Brie liked the rumble of the motor and the wind whipping through her hair. She felt a bit wild and stared at Faelan shamelessly.

He drove her to a side of town she hadn't visited before. The community was made up of young professionals and had an energized feel to it. He pulled up to a small duplex and helped her out of the car.

A jogger passed by and waved. "Hey, Wallace, hot date?"

Blue Eyes gave him a friendly nod and responded, "Something like that."

The man called back, "Don't do anything I wouldn't do."

Faelan leaned down and growled in her ear, "Oh, but I plan to."

She shivered as he led her to his home. This was not the mild-mannered business student she knew from the Center.

His place was small, but filled with modern conveniences. It had a youthful feel. Brie watched him casually fling his keys on a hallway table and motion her to his side.

He said gruffly, "Kneel."

She basked in the feeling of his dominance as she knelt before him and he placed his hand on her head. He spoke solemnly. "Tonight you will serve me well."

Her loins tingled with pleasure and anticipation. "Yes, Faelan."

"Take everything off but your panties."

She started untying the corset, but her hands fumbled with the laces. The way he was staring at her made it feel like her first time. *Calm down!* she commanded herself. She had at least four days more training than he did. That made her the veteran. She stood there confidently with her clothes in a neat pile at her feet, waiting for his next order.

"Turn around slowly."

She felt the intensity of his gaze on every inch of her body. It was disconcerting how wet it made her.

"Go to the chair in the center of the room."

She walked over slowly and faced him, keeping her eyes on his black marble floor.

He came over and showed her the rope in his hand. "I will be tying you to the chair. It will not feel comfortable. I want you to embrace the discomfort and know that you are doing it for me."

She felt butterflies in her stomach. He was not going to be as easy to please as she had initially assumed. Ms. Clark's voice rang in her head. *You know what they say about assuming...*

"Lay your shoulders on top of the back rest and keep your body in a straight line. I will support you until you are properly situated."

Faelan helped her settle her shoulders on top of the wooden back, telling her to put her hands behind her. "Head back. Straighten your body."

The chair dug into her skin and muscles as she

braced her feet against the floor and made her body straight as an arrow. "Beautiful," he said, running his hands down the length of her body. He tied her ankles together and attached them to the legs of the chair. It gave her some support and she was grateful for it. The crease of her ass lay against the edge of the seat and dug into her there, as well.

He tied her wrists together next and attached them to the rungs at the back. This also provided additional support, giving her a chance to remain in this position longer than she could have on her own.

Faelan tied a blindfold over her eyes next, then moved away from her. He said from the other side of the room, "You are beautiful, blossom."

She could feel the emptiness engulf her when he left, and she worried that he was going to leave her like this. For a second she contemplated relaxing, but immediately dismissed it. She lay against the chair, keeping her stomach muscles taut to keep herself in place.

She felt a deep sense of relief when she heard him return. "Did you miss me, blossom?"

"Yes, Faelan." She was surprised how much she meant those simple words.

"We are going to play a game, you and I."

Her heart rate sped up. What could he possibly have in mind with her tied in such a vulnerable position?

"It's a guessing game." Brie heard his footsteps as he walked across the room and stood over her. She couldn't stop her quick, shallow breaths as she waited, feeling completely at his mercy.

Brie jumped when she felt the touch of something

bitterly cold on her chest. It melted on her skin as he rubbed it over both breasts, making her nipples ache in response.

"What is it?"

"Ice, Faelan."

"Very good."

He took the ice away, and then kissed and licked her nipples, returning the warmth he had stolen from her. Then she heard him pick up a new item and felt something cold again. It glided over her stomach, but did not melt. She shook her head, unable to place what it was.

"Don't move," he said smoothly, then turned the item on its side so she could feel its sharpness. She gasped in fear and surprise.

"What is it?"

"A knife, Faelan."

"Yes." He chuckled lightly. The edge of the knife slowly glided down to her mound. She remained perfectly still, holding her breath. He cut through her thong and she felt him pull it away from her body. The flat of the knife returned and slid down over her clit, then the touch disappeared. She allowed herself to breathe then.

"Are you scared, blossom?"

"Yes, Faelan. A little…"

"Good."

His answer gave her goose bumps. He was like a wild animal—enticing, but with the potential to bite her when she least expected it. Why it turned her on, she couldn't explain.

She gasped when she felt his hot breath on her clit. His tongue sought out her sensitive nodule and began caressing it with its moist warmth, while his fingers made their way between her swollen lips. He lifted his mouth from her and said, "Your body gives you away, blossom. I can tell how much you're enjoying my game."

She could not deny it. "Yes, Faelan."

His mouth claimed her clit again. She struggled not to lose her pose as his tongue plundered her. Eventually she cried out, her body shaking from the effort to remain still.

Faelan's tongue left her clit, but his fingers immediately replaced it while his lips slowly made their way up her trembling stomach to her breasts, finally trailing up her neck all the way to her mouth. He kissed her then, and all other awareness fell away. Her only reality was the passion flowing through his lips.

Just as it had the first time, Faelan's kiss took her breath away. The feeling frightened Brie because of the intensity—his kisses were demanding and all-encompassing. When he finally broke away, she groaned.

"Back to the game."

This time she felt something smooth and extremely warm, almost hot. She had no idea what the item was as he glided it over her skin, but it seemed long and cylindrical.

"What is it?"

"I'm not sure, Faelan."

"Maybe this will help."

He trailed the hot cylinder down to her pussy. She whimpered when he separated her outer lips and slid the tip in. The heat of it felt delightfully erotic.

"What is it?" he asked.

"A dildo?"

She heard his chuckle again. "I prefer phallus, but yes, it's a glass dildo, my sweet." He repositioned himself before sliding the hot device inside her. She moaned, having no ability to participate, only receive.

"I put it in hot water to heat the glass, blossom." He pushed it farther inside. The smoothness of the glass was delicious and the warmth of the phallus was like nothing she'd experienced before. He began stroking her with it, while his tongue plundered her mouth again.

His lips stole her breath away as he claimed her pussy with the glass cock in his hand. Brie's body relented to the fire he was creating. She shuddered as sweat dripped from her forehead.

He changed the angle of the toy and it caused her whole body to stiffen. "Come, blossom."

The swirl of erotic emotions gelled into an enormous orgasm. "Oh, Faelan…" she whispered as it took her, claimed her. It was so erotically intense, she couldn't breathe and felt herself blacking out.

She felt him tugging at her bindings as he quickly untied them and took off the blindfold. Soon she was in Faelan's arms. "Are you okay?"

She opened her mouth and then shut it, unable to form words yet. She just nodded.

"What is your color?"

She could hear the worry in his voice and nodded her head again.

He swept his hair away from his eyes in a nervous gesture. His newness was showing, but she found it appealing and attempted a weak smile.

He raised his eyebrow and said accusingly, "Do you normally orgasm like that?"

She shook her head.

His face broke out in a grin. "Ah, then I must be good." He suddenly had the look of a cocky boy with that satisfied half-grin on his face. If she had not been acting as his submissive, she would have rolled her eyes in response.

He must have read her thoughts, because he grabbed her chin. "Oh no, disrespect is not allowed." He pushed her head towards his cock. "Suck me, slower than you have ever sucked a man."

She was still a little disconcerted from her orgasm, but she dutifully got in a kneeling position and opened her mouth. He eased his cock between her lips and she began fellatio.

"Too fast."

She slowed down, licking his frenulum with less vigor.

"Still too fast."

She looked up at him with his cock still in her mouth. Was he trying to test her? She licked his shaft centimeter by slow centimeter, her concentration focused solely on his manhood. Everything else disappeared as she centered on pleasing him.

She felt his hand on her head. "That's better, blossom."

With that simple act, she was totally his submissive again. She moaned with his cock in her mouth, wanting to express her pleasure at being his for the day. She took delight in teasing his manhood and feeling it respond in her mouth—the taste of his pre-come, the warmth of the blood rushing to the area, his rigidness, the little jumps it made in her mouth when she hit just the right spot.

His hand guided her to a faster pace, and she understood he was going to allow her to swallow his essence. "Taste your Master's pleasure," he said, grabbing both sides of her head as he released his seed into her mouth. She swallowed rapidly, surprised that it had a fresh tang, not as bitter as most she had tasted. She held on to his shaft as she finished licking the entirety of it.

"That was good. Now stand before me."

She gracefully stood up. His finger lifted her chin up and his crystal eyes gazed directly into hers. "Who is in charge of you?"

She bowed her head. "You are, Faelan."

He lifted her chin again. "I may not have the experience of the other Doms *yet*, but I know parts of you they cannot. We are kindred spirits, you and I."

She met his confident stare with trepidation. "I have no idea what you're talking about."

"You fight against it, but you cannot hide from me."

Faelan let go of her chin and started moving the chair and other instruments from the room. Then he turned to her. "I will show you what I mean, right now. Stand in the center and face the opposite wall."

She turned away from him and stood there with a mixture of curiosity and anxiety.

To her surprise, he turned on the stereo. The music that erupted from the speakers had a driving beat, full of deep bass and drums. "Dance," he commanded.

Brie felt a little silly, but she started wiggling her ass

to the beat.

"No, close your eyes and give yourself over to the music."

She closed her eyes as he'd commanded. She hadn't heard music like it before. The beat demanded her movement, and the bass drove its vibrations straight to her loins. She relaxed and allowed it to carry her.

"That's it, blossom…"

His praise heightened her pleasure as she danced for Faelan. The bass vibrated in her core, the electronic notes highlighting the score as she moved instinctually to the erotic rhythm.

Goose bumps rose on her skin when she felt his hot breath upon her shoulder. He pressed against her and started moving with her. The two gyrated together as a single unit, in time with the sensual beat. She looked down at his masculine arm wrapped around her waist, struck by how intensely male he was.

He moved away from her and ordered her to continue dancing. She did so reluctantly, wanting Faelan to continue his physical seduction of her. She closed her eyes again and moved to the rhythm, swaying her hips and moving her arms gracefully above her head, feeling totally, utterly *female*.

Her nipples hardened as she felt his naked skin pressing against her, his firm cock tucked between her ass cheeks. Then she felt warm liquid down her front, and the scent of milk chocolate filled her nostrils. Her eyes popped open. She looked down and watched his chocolate-covered hands make dark trails over her white skin.

"Keep dancing," he murmured.

They moved in sync with the music as he covered her chest in warm chocolate. He left for a second and then returned, his hands dripping with more of the sweet ambrosia. She put her hands over his and followed them as they trailed down her stomach and then moved to her waist, grabbing her aggressively. She laid her head back against his shoulder, giving in to the warm sensation of his chocolate caress.

He panted in her ear like an animal. Then she felt his masculine hand grasp her throat, holding her possessively. She was overcome by the gesture, loving the submissive emotion it provoked. "Release your animal, blossom," he growled. He then pushed two fingers into her mouth and she started sucking them as they continued to grind to the music.

When the beat slowed, Faelan turned her around and pushed Brie to her knees, then joined her on the floor. He cupped her breasts in his hands and squeezed them together before licking and biting her chocolate flesh. Brie moaned raggedly, but her voice could not compete with the loud music filling her senses. The driving rhythm made her feel young, reckless, wild… She scratched her chocolaty fingernails down his chest. She looked down at his long, hard cock and cried, "I need…"

His lustful stare melted her loins. He turned her away from him, forcing her onto her hands and knees. Faelan grabbed her buttocks roughly, sexually, with only one thought in mind—to impale her with his manhood. She growled with animal passion as he delivered a powerful thrust. The two of them fucked to the aggressive beat of the music. His thrusts were demanding and she met every stroke by pushing against him, driving him in deeper. Needing more…

He sensed her unspoken desire and pushed her to the cold marble, shoving his cock deeper. She closed her eyes and accepted all of him. *Possess me!*

The two of them grunted as they copulated on the floor—and copulated was the proper term. She *was* lust—hungry, insatiable, ravenous. He met that un-quenchable need, fucking her hard, picking her up and pushing her against walls, tables, chairs… He was rough with her, pulling her hair, grabbing her forcefully, slamming his cock into her repeatedly.

And her body took his raw passion—*craved* it, in fact. She licked his sweaty skin, needing to taste every part of him. At one point, the need for him became so intense that she bit down on his shoulder. He growled in lusty encouragement, pressing her against him.

By the time they had finished, she was a quivering heap of feminine flesh. She had to hold on to Faelan as he lathered her up and rinsed her off in the shower. Then he carried her to his bed and gathered her in his arms, panting softly in her ear. They lay like that for what seemed like hours, her body taking its own sweet time to come back down.

"You smell delicious," he said huskily.

She buried her face in his neck and took a long in-hale. She smiled as she looked into his blue eyes. "You have an intoxicating smell yourself."

He pressed her closer to him and chuckled.

"What's so funny?"

"I remember that day you were pushed into my chest at the door. I knew by the way you stiffened that you felt the connection too, no matter how much you wanted to fight it."

"May I speak freely?" Brie asked.

"Yes, blossom."

"You are an arrogant man."

"I think you confuse arrogance with confidence, my sweet," he said, kissing the top of her head.

She smiled despite herself. For being as green as he was, the man was Dom through and through.

"You and I are a lot alike, you know."

She looked at him doubtfully. "How so?"

Faelan swept a string of wet hair from her cheek. "We both run on natural instinct. But it's not just our instincts that we have in common, it's also the burning desire to experience the limitless possibilities. Imagine two people determined to explore each other. Nothing too mundane or extreme to be considered, as long as both consent."

Her heart quickened at the thought.

He kissed her tenderly on the lips and murmured, "I bet you didn't know that I'm taking private lessons on top of my training."

She shook her head and sat up to look at him more closely, surprised by the revelation. It seemed his interest in domination was not simply an infatuation over a girl. He was taking his training as seriously as she was—*more so, in fact.*

"I've decided to get the most out of the break from

my business classes. Not wasting time while I have the opportunity to learn from the best." Brie nodded, feeling a new level of respect for the man. She was about to tell him so when he switched gears on her, gliding his index finger leisurely down the middle of her chest.

"Now that I have brought out the lioness, I want to hear you purr." His mouth demanded her attention as his hands began their wicked exploration. Brie wiggled and squirmed, thoroughly enjoying the fruits of his training.

When Faelan dropped her off at the Center, he insisted on not only escorting her inside, but also directing her to the chair next to Mary. He bent over and bit her earlobe. It sent a fresh set of shivers down her spine. He chuckled softly before leaving her side.

Mary gave Brie a strange look, so she mumbled, "What's your problem?" Mary ignored her and turned back to the panel.

Brie wondered if Mary had struggled with Captain. It would be a shame for both parties, but Mary shouldn't be taking it out on her.

Once Lea joined the group, the panel discussion began. Brie was relieved to hear via the trainers' questions that Mary had had a positive experience with Captain. Surprisingly, Mary had actually enjoyed her time with him. It seemed that she'd relished being chained to the bed even more than Brie had. Maybe her calling was to be a pet for a strong Dom who could balance discipline with tenderness.

Lea's last Auction Day had been with a Dom named 'the Sheik'. He'd had a harem of five girls that he'd introduced Lea to. From the glow on her face and the excitement in her voice, it was easy to tell it had been Lea's dream come true.

Sir turned his attention to Brie last. "How would you rate your time with Mr. Wallace?"

"I would give today a solid nine."

"Really?" he asked. "I couldn't help noticing the marks on your arms."

Mary stared at her again, and this time Brie could not miss the look of jealousy that played across her face.

Brie examined both arms and saw that there were several red splotches, some of which were beginning to turn purple. She'd had no idea they'd been that rough. She looked back at him and said, "It was worth it, Sir."

"What exactly did you do?" Marquis asked, clearly interested.

"Umm…basic, animalistic sex. We did play a game first. A guessing game that included a blindfold and certain items I had to identify."

"I wouldn't have suspected you liked it that rough, Miss Bennett," Master Anderson commented.

"I'm a bit surprised myself."

Sir followed up by asking, "Based on your rating, I assume it's something you would entertain again?"

She blushed and stammered, "Ah…only with the right Dom, Sir."

He answered with a simple, "I see," but the way he

said it was odd. She wasn't sure how to take those two words, and was surprised when all five trainers wrote down something on their paper.

Ms. Clark asked the standard question: "Is there anything you would change about the encounter?"

Brie answered with a straight face, "Well, having a rug would have been nice. The marble was a bit hard."

Mary snickered softly, causing Ms. Clark to instantly turn on her. "Do not encourage such insolence!"

Ms. Clark ordered Brie to look her in the face. Brie felt queasy as she lifted her eyes to the Domme's. The look of disgust and anger was hard to take.

"Such a flippant answer has only one recourse—the stockade."

Brie silently groaned. It was true. She had not treated Ms. Clark with the respect she was due, but this was their last auction night together. All Brie wanted to do was head out of the door with Mary and Lea.

"Please, Mistress Clark. I'm sorry if I sounded flippant."

"You did not *sound* flippant, you *were* flippant. Speak again and I will increase your punishment."

Brie nodded and sighed inwardly. She hoped desperately that the other two would wait for her. She needed her time with them.

Master Coen addressed the group. "This was your last auction. Next week, we will be introducing you to the community. It is a formal affair. I advise you to buy clothes suitable for the occasion."

"What sort of clothes, Master Coen?" Mary asked.

"Clothes that would please a potential Master, of

course."

His words made Brie's heart stop for a second. *My Master...*

Marquis Gray spoke next. "You will have the option to present a symbolic collar to the Dom of your choice, but keep two things in mind. One, you do not have to pick a Dom. In fact, we would discourage it. It would be wise to give yourself time to circulate. Second, even if you are certain you have found the Dominant you wish to partner with, he has the right to refuse you."

Brie's jaw dropped.

Marquis continued, "To prevent that from happening, we will allow you to meet with up to three Doms during the gathering. If, at the end of the night, you still want to present your collar, you will be given the chance to do so."

Sir added, "Whether you choose to present your collar or not, take advantage of the three meetings. It is an opportunity to quiz Dominants you are interested in, and you are allowed to engage in private activities, if you so desire. You will have no better chance to interview potential partners."

It kind of reminded Brie of speed dating, with a BDSM twist.

"Are there any questions?" Sir asked.

Lea spoke up. "Can we change our minds partway through the night if we decide not to present the collar?"

"At any point you may change your mind. This is a personal decision. Do not feel pressured—it's simply an opportunity afforded you at the ceremony."

There was no question in Brie's mind about presenting a collar. She was desperate to commit to one Dom, but the problem was she wasn't sure which one yet. Having her heart stretched in so many directions was killing her inside.

"If there are no further questions, you are dismissed."

"All except you, Miss Bennett," Ms. Clark snapped.

Brie stood up to follow, but Marquis accosted Ms. Clark and spoke to her briefly. While she was waiting, Brie heard Lea whisper, "We'll be in the parking lot."

Brie closed her eyes in relief. At least Ms. Clark wasn't taking that away from her. The Domme snapped her fingers and gestured for Brie to follow. Her trainer's heels clicked loudly down the hall. The ire in her walk was easy to hear, filling Brie with apprehension.

Why am I such an idiot?

A Little Female Persuasion

Her trainer opened a door to a classroom Brie hadn't been inside. It was completely bare except for the stockade in the center. "Place yourself in it, Miss Bennett, while I ready your punishment."

Brie knelt down next to the ugly wooden device. She gingerly put her hands and neck into the grooves and stayed there while Ms. Clark busied herself. Brie had to keep the tears from falling when her trainer lowered the top board down. The click of the lock solidified Brie's disgrace.

"Five weeks I have had to put up with your insolence. This has been a long time in coming."

"I'm sorry, Ms. Clark."

"Mistress to you," she corrected. "Save your apologies. They have no place here. You have been disrespectful to your trainer and must be punished. It is a natural consequence for disobedience."

Ms. Clark pulled Brie's skirt and panties off. Brie felt Ms. Clark's hands spread her outer lips apart. "You will wear this for the entire session. I don't think I need to tell you that coming is not an option." Brie felt the cool invasion of a dildo push into her opening. She bit her lip, feeling nothing but humiliation.

Her Mistress turned the vibrator on to its fastest setting, then she showed Brie a long wooden paddle. "I prefer to use a cane, but Marquis forbade it with you."

Brie was grateful for his intervention. It would have ruined the instrument for her.

When Mistress moved behind Brie, she closed her eyes. All she wanted was to escape the experience and she tried to shut down emotionally. It was as if Mistress knew, because she announced, "You will count for me, Miss Bennett."

"Yes, Mistress."

"Normally, I tell my subs the number of hits they must endure. However, I think I will keep that to myself."

Brie groaned silently. The paddle came down hard across both cheeks. Brie gasped as the sting of it burst over her skin, and then dissipated. "One," she called out to Mistress.

It was immediately followed by another, equally hard swat. Brie choked out, "Two."

"Why are you being punished tonight, Miss Bennett?"

"I made a joke instead of answering your question."

The third hit landed on her tender ass and Brie felt the first tear fall.

"It was your lack of respect towards me that was the problem." Ms. Clark waited.

Brie realized she'd forgotten to count and blurted,

"Three."

"You will receive an extra for forgetting."

Brie knew better than to beg for mercy, but had to bite her lip to prevent it.

"All along I have striven to help you succeed as a submissive, and yet you return my gift with flippancy?" The fourth swat made Brie weak all over.

"Four, Mistress."

"What is your greatest weakness?"

Brie thought Mistress was taking a breather until she felt the fifth land on her ass. She gasped in surprise. "Five… I look Dominants in the eyes, Mistress."

The sixth came with a hearty, "No!" Tears fell down Brie's cheeks; there was no holding them back any longer. "Your greatest weakness is not remembering you are a submissive when you are in the presence of Dominants."

"Six," Brie said meekly.

"If that was foremost in your mind, you would not fail constantly."

Brie tried to silence her sob. "Thank you, Mistress."

Mistress rubbed the paddle over her ass, making it sting from the contact. "I have never seen such talent wrapped up in such foolishness." She slapped the paddle with a little less muscle.

"Seven." Brie held her breath. *Is Mistress giving me a compliment?*

"From this day forward, you will not forget your place." She swung the paddle hard, and Brie's ass burst into burning heat.

"Eight…Yes, Mistress."

Brie heard the paddle drop to the floor. Mistress bent over and played with her vibrating clit. Brie had forgotten about the dildo inside her until the Domme had started manipulating it.

"I want you to stay here in the dark and concentrate on what you have learned tonight. I shouldn't have to repeat it, but coming is not allowed." She pulled the dildo out a little farther so that the clitoral stimulator attached to it vibrated more fully against Brie's aching clit.

Mistress stood up and asked, "What do you say, Miss Bennett?"

"Thank you, Mistress."

"It's been my pleasure."

She walked out of the room, flicking off the light switch before she left, leaving Brie alone in the dark.

The throbbing of her buttocks started pulsing with her clit. Faelan came to mind. She recalled the lusty way he had taken her and had to fight off the feelings building up.

No! She shook her head. She dug down deep and pushed away all thoughts of pleasure. Endurance and obedience were her only goals; they were the only things that mattered. She was determined not to get herself into this situation again. After what felt like several excruciating hours, Mistress returned.

"Did you come?" she asked calmly.

"No, Mistress."

"Fine." Ms. Clark pulled out the dildo and unfastened the stockade. "Get dressed. You may leave."

Brie slowly pulled her panties back on and zipped up

her skirt. She walked out of the Center with her head held high but her butt cheeks throbbing. She'd survived Ms. Clark's punishment and learned a valuable lesson from it.

Both girls approached her when she went to unlock her car. Lea put her hand on Brie's shoulder and asked, "How are you?"

Brie gave a faint smile. "Okay. My ass hurts like the dickens, but I'll live."

"That bitch beat you while you were in the stockade?" Mary asked, clearly upset.

"Yes, but I survived and am better for it."

"What do you mean?" Mary barked, looking like she wanted to kick some Ms. Clark butt.

Brie hemmed and hawed before she answered. "Ms. Clark was right to punish me. I was not respectful."

"Fuck me! I can't believe you're being such a wuss. That woman has been nothing but a bitch to you."

Brie looked Mary in the eye. "I have not been submissive to her."

Mary shook her head in disbelief.

Lea took Brie's hand and squeezed it. "Yes."

Brie looked at Lea in surprise. All this time she had thought of Lea as the lesser sub, but had been blind to the girl's strengths. Lea might not have had the same level of book smarts, but it was obvious that she had her own unique talents as a submissive. There was a reason that Ms. Clark had praised her and other Doms had rated her well. *What a fool I've been,* Brie thought, giving Lea a quick hug.

She announced to both girls, "We are headed to my

home. This is our last auction debrief and we are partying all night long!"

Brie eagerly opened her apartment to her friends,
proud of the array of drinks and foods she had accumu-
lated for the occasion. It was every bit as extravagant as
the spread they'd had at the Center, and had taken weeks
to save up for. She also had her camera ready.

Mary eyed it suspiciously. "I am *not* going to interview for you."

"You don't have to," Brie assured her. "I just want
to record our evening. I'll edit it later and let you look it
over. I promise I won't use any footage you aren't
comfortable with. I just want us to enjoy ourselves
without worrying about the camera."

"Hey, I'm totally down with that," Lea said, going
over to the lens and blowing a kiss.

Brie grinned. "Thanks, girlfriend."

"Oh, is that how it is? You playing favorites, Miss
Bennett?" Mary snarked.

"Only if you won't agree to being filmed."

"Blackmail."

Brie bumped hips with her playfully. "The blackmail-
iest."

"Bitch."

"The bitchiest."

Mary swatted her ass lightly, causing Brie to squeal in
pain. "Okay, fine, Miss Bennett, but I have final say."

Brie moved a safe distance away before answering, "I
wouldn't have it any other way, Mary Quite Contrary."

Brie herded her friends to her couch with their favorite drinks and snacks. She sat down gingerly, finding the

position that hurt the least. The three spent the night sharing not only the details of their last Auction Day, but their favorite moments from their time at the Center.

"My favorite has to be the violet wand," Lea blurted.

"Not your outing with Ms. Clark?" Mary asked sarcastically.

"Well, that was exceptional. However, that wand… I'm telling you, I haven't felt anything like it."

"What about you?" Brie asked Mary.

Mary instantly clammed up and stared at the camera.

"It won't bite, woman. Pretend it's not there and tell me what you liked."

Mary took a deep breath. She turned away from the camera before she spoke. "Hmm… So much to choose from. You have to admit we are the luckiest women alive. So many Doms and so many scenarios to reflect on."

"True," Brie agreed, "but which was your favorite?"

"Oh, hell… Marquis Gray."

Brie and Lea nodded in unison. Lea grinned. "Totally makes sense. He is a master of the flogger."

"I do like Marquis…" Brie said dreamily.

"I would ask that man to collar me if it was allowed," Mary said, taking a sip of her drink.

Brie felt a cold chill. *Allowed?* Mary must not know what she was talking about. The waiting was almost over… Once they'd graduated from the course, the trainers would be fair game.

Mary shocked Brie again when she added, "But I sure would like to take a spin with Faelan."

Brie felt her hackles instantly rise. "Why?"

"He's the talk of the Center. Haven't you heard? All of his subs want to partner with him. Damn, I want a chance at that boy! There's something about those eyes that drives me absolutely wild. I haven't stopped dreaming about Todd Wallace since suffering through his vibrator punishment. I can't explain what it is about him, but I am majorly attracted."

What is Mary's problem? Does she have to lust after every guy I like? Brie got up to fix another drink to avoid saying something she'd regret.

Lea spoke up. "He's been Brie's since even before Brie knew he existed."

Mary turned on her. "I don't understand it. What does she have that I don't?"

"A heart," Lea joked.

Brie headed back with a new drink in her hand. She shook her head in response to Lea's statement. "No, Mary has a heart." She looked at her former nemesis. "You were kind to Captain tonight."

Mary's eyes softened. "He's a good man."

Brie smiled, agreeing, "Yes, he is." She paused for a moment, debating whether she should voice her thoughts, but forged ahead anyway. "I doubted you, Mary. But I should have known better. Underneath that hard exterior is a beautiful person."

"Shut the fuck up!" Mary glared at the camera accusingly. "Turn that damn thing off!"

Brie didn't budge. "Why? The truth pissing you off?"

Mary suddenly looked close to tears. Brie rushed over to her camera and switched it off. "I didn't mean anything by it…" She added tenderly, "Bitch."

Mary looked her in the eye and mouthed the word, "Thanks."

Brie suddenly understood that Mary wasn't used to compliments from other women. "I only speak the truth, you know."

Mary began wiping tears away as quickly as they appeared.

Lea looked at Brie in shock, clearly not knowing how to handle the situation. "So Mary, I don't suppose you've heard that a good submissive is hard to beat?"

Mary shook her head a couple of times and then started laughing hysterically, far more enthusiastically than the joke deserved. But it prompted both girls to join her. Brie poured Mary another drink and handed Lea a beer.

She held up her wine glass and toasted, "May we go down in the history books as the best damn submissive class known in the history of the Submissive Training Center!"

They held up their glasses one at a time, each girl cheering for herself:

"Lea the Lovely!"

"Mary the Magnificent!"

"Brie the Bodacious!"

They broke out in more peals of laughter until Mr. Nguyen hammered from the floor above. Brie looked at the clock. "Oh, crap, girls, we have to try to keep it down. I'm pissing off my neighbor because it's four o'clock in the morning."

There was silence for a couple of seconds, and then the snickers began. Mary smiled at Brie and suggested,

"Why don't we pay a visit to Mr. Nguyen and show him what we've learned?"

Brie started crying as she tried to hold back the laughter threatening to spill out. She stumbled over to the other two and wrapped them in her arms. "I love you guys."

Lea hugged back, but Mary pulled away. "Enough with the hugging. You are not hot in any way, shape or form."

Brie laughed out loud. "Whatever, Mary the Mediocre."

"Magnificent, bitch."

Brie held her hand up in a dismissive manner. "Whatever…"

Mary tackled her to the ground and Lea jumped on top.

Brie grinned up at the ceiling. Five weeks ago, she had been alone and bored. Now she had these two amazing women as friends *and* a whole exotic world to explore with the Dom of her choice.

Truly, life doesn't get better than this…

The End Approaches

Even though it was nearly five a.m., the girls were still partying hard. Five weeks of submissive training meant they had a lot to celebrate. Mary had even given Brie permission to turn the camera back on so that she could record their conversation for her documentary.

"But if you dare get mushy on me, that thing is trash," Mary warned, pointing to Brie's movie camera.

"Got it. I promise to treat you like the heartless bitch you are, Mary," Brie joked.

"Fine. See that you do."

Lea jumped on the couch and asked, "So, Brie, are you really going to pick a Master on graduation day?"

"Absolutely. My heart has been torn into pieces. For my sanity, I need to give myself to one Dom." She nudged Lea with her shoulder. "How about you?"

Her best friend's ample chest turned a deep shade of red, along with her face. Brie knew something was up. "What's going on?"

Lea fiddled with her corset as she talked. "Ms. Clark kind of suggested I might be a good candidate for their

Dom training."

"What! You, a Dom?"

Lea broke out in giggles. "No, silly. I would help the Doms practice."

"You have got to be kidding!" Mary shouted.

Brie gave her the evil eye. The last thing she needed was Mr. Nguyen knocking on her door and telling her to keep it down.

Mary frowned at her, but spoke softly to Lea. "You with all those Doms-in-training? In your dreams… They'll never accept you."

Lea stuck her chin up. "Shows how much you know. I've already been accepted. I start in two weeks."

"Fuck me!" Mary snapped. "How did you manage that?"

Lea grinned. "It pays to be nice."

Brie shook her head. "Damn girl, you're lucky. Wish Ms. Clark liked me…"

Mary huffed angrily. "What some people won't do to get what they want."

Brie tugged on a lock of her blonde hair. "You're just jealous. I can totally see you going down on Ms. Clark if you thought it would get you what you wanted."

"Yeah, well you tried it, and see how far it got you." Mary raised her eyebrow. "And just what do you think I want anyway, Miss Know-It-All?"

Brie looked her over carefully. "I think you are more like me than you want to admit. I bet you're chomping at the bit to be collared by some hunky Dom, but you're too chicken."

Mary snorted in disgust. "Ha! Shows how much you

know. There is no way I would settle down with one Master. Not when I have a whole world of Dominants yet to be explored." She waved Brie off dismissively. "I think you're an idiot."

"Oh, don't hold back. Tell me what you really think," Brie said, laughing.

Mary sat down next to her, suddenly looking serious. "No, you shouldn't let anyone collar you at the graduation ceremony. You've had so little experience. There are way better Doms out there."

"Are you kidding me? The Submissive Training Center attracts the very best. I'm confident I've already met my Master… I just haven't decided which one."

"Well, like I said, you are a fool." Mary got up to mix herself a drink.

Lea put her hand on Brie's shoulder. "Even though Mary is socially inept, I agree with her, Brie. You should live a little before you settle down."

"Et tu, Brute?" Brie complained. "I don't think either of you understand how hard this has been on me. I *need* to serve one Dom. It gets so intense sometimes, I feel like I can't breathe."

Lea wrapped her arms around her. "If that's how you feel, then I'm behind you one hundred percent. Besides, I'm curious about the collaring ceremony. It sounds so damn romantic!"

Mary came back into the room. "It's not romantic. It's more like a business transaction."

Brie rolled her eyes. "You have no idea what you are talking about. I imagine it being as romantic as a wedding, but with a sexy element because of the D/s relationship." She literally shivered just thinking about handing her collar over to her Master.

"I go back to my original observation. You *are* an idiot."

Brie shot back, "And I go back to mine. You're just jealous!"

Lea put her arms around both women. "Girls, girls, no need to bicker. Tell me, what did the naughty sub say to her Master?"

Brie took the bait, knowing Lea was only trying to help. "Okay, what did the naughty sub say to her Master?"

"'Who died and left you in charge?'"

On that humorous note, the celebration ended. Brie watched her friends walk to their cars and felt a momentary stab of pain. *This is it. Our last week of training…*

Lea turned around and yelled, "We're going to hang after graduation, right?"

Brie blushed. "Well, maybe not *right* after graduation. But soon, I promise!"

"I'm holding you to that, Stinky Cheese," Mary shouted.

"You do that, Mary the Mediocre!"

Mary gave her the bird. Brie laughed to herself as she shut the door. *Man, I love my friends!*

That Monday, the girls met in the commons and lined up in front of the panel waiting for them. Unfortunately, they were met with frowns.

Sir stood up and chastised them harshly. "Did I not assign you rituals to be performed before each session?" All three girls bowed their heads in shame. Brie had completely forgotten about it over the weekend.

Mary immediately went to bow on the floor, but Sir stopped her. "Too late. You are not allowed the privilege now." He added, in a severe but quiet tone that pierced Brie's shamed heart, "Do not forget again."

He went on to explain the layout of their last week before handing each girl an individual schedule for the night. Brie's first task would be to write down general questions for the Doms she would interview on graduation day. Sir announced that he would meet with her afterwards so they could go over her questions together. She could barely contain her excitement.

When Brie had finished her long list of questions, she got up and started towards Sir's office. He met her halfway down the hallway and directed her back to the commons. She wondered why, but dutifully followed behind Sir.

They sat down at a table across from each other. Sir looked deliciously hot in his white button-up shirt, which was rolled up at the sleeves as if he was ready for business. She tried to avoid looking into his intense eyes, as she knew they would render her speechless if she dared to peek.

Although it was a mock interview, Brie felt frightfully nervous, as if she were really interviewing Sir as her potential Dom. He could sense that, or it was written all over her face, because the first thing he said was, "You can calm down now, Miss Bennett. I'm simply going over your questions with you."

She felt her whole body flush and picked up her paper in self-defense, beginning with her first question.

"How old are you, Sir?"

He nodded. "That's an acceptable question."

She stared at him. When he didn't answer, she asked, "So?"

"What? You want me to answer that?"

"Please, Sir. It'll help me excel when I do the real thing."

He raised his eyebrow, but acquiesced. "Thirty-three."

"I see…" She quickly did the math and realized he was eleven years older. She imagined Sir as an eleven-year-old boy, holding her in his arms as a tiny little infant. It was an amusing image, and she snorted.

"Yes?"

Brie bit her lip and looked back down at her paper. "How long have you been a Dominant?"

"A fine question. Gives you an idea of their experience level."

She rested her chin on her hand while she waited for his reply.

He growled in irritation, but she could tell he was amused. "Miss Bennett, is this really necessary?"

"It is, Sir. I am going to be making an important decision, maybe the most important decision of my life, and I need to feel prepared. Just going over my list of questions isn't going to make me feel confident about the interviews later this week."

He stared at her for several seconds before answering. "I've taken the lifestyle seriously for eight years now."

"Thank you." Brie put the paper up to her face so he

couldn't see her smile. "Hmm… Do you like animals?"

"What?"

She put the paper back down. "I've heard that Doms who like animals are more likely to treat their subs well."

"What, did you google that?"

She looked sideways, blushing at his sarcasm. "Of course."

"Scratch it off your list. You only have thirty minutes per interview, so keep it simple and to the point."

Brie crossed out the question and moved to the next. "What made you decide to pursue the Dominant life-style?"

"A worthwhile question." He looked her directly in the eye. Did he know she had trouble concentrating when he did that? "In my twenties I realized I had a natural affinity for discovering a woman's unspoken desires." He smiled at her, and Brie stopped breathing due to its sheer radiance. "In case you're curious, I was not abused growing up, nor do I take pleasure in beating women. I simply enjoy exploring a woman's sexuality to its fullest."

Please, Sir, explore mine!

Brie forced herself to breathe. "Are you interested in a twenty-four seven, total power exchange or a casual relationship?"

"Important question to ask. However, I am not in-terested in a relationship at this time, Miss Bennett."

Brie prodded him, "Fine, but if you *were*…"

"A full-time relationship."

She was happy to hear it. "If you could change one thing about yourself, what would it be and why?"

"Scratch that."

Brie dutifully crossed it out without an argument. "Classical or rock?"

"Irrelevant. Scratch it off your list as well."

"What do you do for a living?"

"Necessary question. I am an administrative consultant."

"Does it pay well?"

Sir cleared his throat. "I have no complaints."

Brie looked at her list and realized he wasn't going to like most of her questions, so she skipped over a majority of them. "What kind of relationship do you have with your mother?"

"Brie."

"What?"

"Simple, to the point. I haven't heard a question about your film career."

"Wait, I have one." She skimmed down the page. "Here it is. How do you feel about your sub working outside the relationship?"

"Ask instead, 'Would you support my career as a film director?'"

"Oh, that's much more direct." She quickly wrote the question down and then waited for his answer.

He gave her an exasperated look, but responded, "I would support such a career choice…not that it matters." He glanced at his watch. "We need to end this session. Go over your questions tonight, make sure they are specific and give you the answers you require. Also, leave room for an intimate encounter with each Dom. Being able to compare three applicants side by side is an unparalleled experience. There have been several past submissives who were able to make a definitive decision after such a comparison."

"Do we have time for that, Sir? For practice purposes, naturally," Brie added with a playful grin.

His eyes suddenly became distant, his voice cold. "I expect you to go over your list tonight and weed out the waste." He handed her a piece of paper. "Here are the vows spoken at a collaring ceremony. I suggest you memorize them." He glanced at his watch again, stating, "It is time you meet with Mr. Gallant. Leave now."

Brie was shaken by the sudden change in him. She nodded meekly as she got up and left the table. The man was an enigma.

ABOUT THE AUTHOR

Over Two Million readers have enjoyed Red's stories

Red Phoenix – USA Today Bestselling Author
Winner of 8 Readers' Choice Awards

Hey Everyone!

I'm Red Phoenix, an author who also happens to be a submissive in real life. I wrote the Brie's Submission series because I wanted people everywhere to know just how much fun BDSM can be.

There is a huge cast of characters who are part of Brie's journey. The further you read into the story the more you learn about each one. I hope you grow to love Brie and the gang as much as I do.

They've become like family.

When I'm not writing, you can find me online with readers.

I heart my fans! ~Red

To find out more visit my Website

redphoenixauthor.com

Follow Me on BookBub

bookbub.com/authors/red-phoenix

Newsletter: Sign up

redphoenixauthor.com/newsletter-signup

Facebook: AuthorRedPhoenix

Twitter: @redphoenix69

Instagram: RedPhoenixAuthor

I invite you to join my reader Group!

facebook.com/groups/539875076052037

SIGN UP FOR MY NEWSLETTER
HERE FOR THE LATEST RED
PHOENIX UPDATES

FOLLOW ME ON INSTAGRAM
INSTAGRAM.COM/REDPHOENIXAUTHOR

SALES, GIVEAWAYS, NEW RELEAS-
ES, PREORDER LINKS, AND MORE!
SIGN UP HERE

REDPHOENIXAUTHOR.COM/NEWSLETTER-
SIGNUP

Red Phoenix is the author of:

Brie's Submission Series:
Teach Me #1
Love Me #2
Catch Me #3
Try Me #4
Protect Me #5
Hold Me #6
Surprise Me #7
Trust Me #8
Claim Me #9
Enchant Me #10
A Cowboy's Heart #11
Breathe with Me #12
Her Russian Knight #13
Under His Protection #14
Her Russian Returns #15
In Sir's Arms #16
Bound by Love #17
Tied to Hope #18
Hope's First Christmas #19
Secrets of the Heart #20

***You can also purchase the** AUDIO BOOK **Versions**

Also part of the Submissive Training Center world:

Rise of the Dominates Trilogy
Sir's Rise #1
Master's Fate #2
The Russian Reborn #3

Captain's Duet
Safe Haven #1
Destined to Dominate #2

Other Books by Red Phoenix

Blissfully Undone
* Available in eBook and paperback

(Snowy Fun—Two people find themselves snowbound in a cabin where hidden love can flourish, taking one couple on a sensual journey into ménage à trois)

His Scottish Pet: Dom of the Ages
* Available in eBook and paperback

Audio Book: *His Scottish Pet: Dom of the Ages*

(Scottish Dom—A sexy Dom escapes to Scotland in the late 1400s. He encounters a waif who has the potential to free him from his tragic curse)

The Erotic Love Story of Amy and Troy
* Available in eBook and paperback

(Sexual Adventures—True love reigns, but fate continually throws Troy and Amy into the arms of others)

eBooks

Varick: The Reckoning

(Savory Vampire—A dark, sexy vampire story. The hero navigates the dangerous world he has been thrust into with lusty passion and a pure heart)

Keeper of the Wolf Clan (Keeper of Wolves, #1)

(Sexual Secrets—A virginal werewolf must act as the clan's mysterious Keeper)

The Keeper Finds Her Mate (Keeper of Wolves, #2)

(Second Chances—A young she-wolf must choose between old ties or new beginnings)

The Keeper Unites the Alphas (Keeper of Wolves, #3)

(Serious Consequences—The young she-wolf is captured by the rival clan)

Boxed Set: Keeper of Wolves Series (Books 1-3)

(Surprising Secrets—A secret so shocking it will rock Layla's world. The young she-wolf is put in a position of being able to save her werewolf clan or becoming the reason for its destruction)

Socrates Inspires Cherry to Blossom

(Satisfying Surrender—A mature and curvaceous woman
becomes fascinated by an online Dom who has much to
teach her)

By the Light of the Scottish Moon

(Saving Love—Two lost souls, the Moon, a werewolf,
and a death wish…)

In 9 Days

(Sweet Romance—A young girl falls in love with the new
student, nicknamed "the Freak")

---

9 Days and Counting

(Sacrificial Love—The sequel to *In 9 Days* delves into the
emotional reunion of two longtime lovers)

And Then He Saved Me

(Saving Tenderness—When a young girl tries to kill
herself, a man of great character intervenes with a love
that heals)

Play With Me at Noon

(Seeking Fulfillment—A desperate wife lives out her
fantasies by taking five different men in five days)

Connect with Red on Substance B

Substance B is a platform for independent authors to directly connect with their readers. Please visit Red's Substance B page where you can:

- Sign up for Red's newsletter
- Send a message to Red
- See all platforms where Red's books are sold

Visit Substance B today to learn more about your favorite independent authors.